"I just wanted to tell you that I'm really not mad at all. I've been acting like an idiot lately."

"Oh, Sandy, that's not true at all." I stopped myself before I blurted out what else was on my mind. Somehow, today, Sandy seemed new and attractive to me, and yet I was sure that he was the same Sandy as always.

Suddenly I felt his hand reach for mine and I gripped his tightly, as if I could communicate how I felt. I turned my face to his, and our lips met in a sweet, lingering kiss.

Dear Readers,

We at Silhouette would like to thank all our readers for your many enthusiastic letters. In direct response to your encouragement, we are now publishing *three* FIRST LOVEs every month.

As always FIRST LOVEs are written especially for and about you—your hopes, your dreams, your ambitions.

Please continue to share your suggestions and comments with us; they play an important part in our pleasing you.

I invite you to write to us at the address below:

Nancy Jackson
Senior Editor
Silhouette Books
P.O. Box 769
New York, N.Y. 10019

LOVE NOTE
Jessica Howell

First Love from Silhouette

Published by Silhouette Books New York

America's Publisher of Contemporary Romance

SILHOUETTE BOOKS, a Simon & Schuster Division of
GULF & WESTERN CORPORATION
1230 Avenue of the Americas, New York, N.Y. 10020

Distributed by Pocket Books

ISBN: 0-671-53337-1

First Silhouette Books printing January, 1983

10 9 8 7 6 5 4 3 2 1

1

"Dreams, dreams, you're in my dreams.
Day and night
You're always in my dreams."

Two figures stood alone on stage singing in a circle of light, their powerful voices filling the plush Broadway theater with perfect harmony. The orchestra in the pit below added another layer of gloss to their performance. Leaning back, trying to relax, I watched the famous singing team of West and Lane, better known to me as Claire and Marty, my parents.

I used to like going to their concerts because it meant I could get all dressed up and stay out late. It was funny to see people making such a fuss over Mom and Dad. Lately the whole thing makes me feel uncomfortable. At home they are still just everyday people, but once on stage they become strangers to me. They seem to expect I'll be at their

5

annual New York concert, though; so rather than make a big deal out of it, I go.

When the song was over, ending their hour-and-a-half concert, the audience jumped to their feet with appreciative applause, the woman next to me, as many others, yelling "bravo" as she clapped. I found myself standing and clapping too, feeling at the same time proud and resentful. A stagehand rushed out and presented Mom with a bouquet of lush red roses. Holding them against her long black gown as she stood next to Dad, in his elegant tuxedo, they both bowed, and Mom, smiling radiantly, threw kisses.

As the ecstatic audience streamed out of the back of the theater, I headed for the front, passed through an obscure door, headed across the huge stage and down a short hall to Mom and Dad's dressing room. Giving the guard outside a familiar nod, I went in.

Dad, already changed into slacks and a shirt, was sitting in a comfortable chair studying some music. Mom was at her dressing table in a robe, her face covered with cream. There were a few other people milling around.

"It was great," I told them both. "The audience loved you."

"What did you think of the new 'Dreams' piece your father wrote?" Mom asked me. "It's going to be our new single."

"Terrific." I answered.

Just then, Seth Guild, their arranger, came up behind me. "What's happening to my little girl?" he demanded, putting his arms around me with a squeeze. He was a good-looking guy about Dad's age. "You're growing into a beauty right in front of my eyes." I wriggled away as fast as I could.

"Mr. Guild, I'm nearly fifteen." This seemed to me to have more clout than just fourteen or fourteen and a half.

"You mean you're old enough to come out to dinner with me?" he murmured, and his arm came around me again. It was creepy.

"Barbara," Mom asked, looking at me in the mirror, "Poke your head out, will you, and let Michael know we'll need the car in ten minutes." Without a word, I was out the door.

Finally saying goodnight to everyone who worked with my folks, just outside the stage door we ran into a crush of people all yelling things: "Miss West, we loved the show." "May we have your autograph please, Mr. Lane?" Hands clutching scraps of paper flew into their faces, and Mom and Dad hurriedly signed whatever they could reach.

Five minutes later, it was a great relief to sit silently in our big brown car with Mom and Dad's chauffeur Michael driving us away from all the fuss. Mom and Dad were always very quiet after their concerts. Whether they were thinking back about their performances or just plain wiped out, I could never tell. For my part, I was relieved to be going home.

My name is Barbara Lane, and though you might think that as the daughter of famous singers my life would be perfect, these days it's been giving me nothing but headaches. I live in a big house on Long Island with my folks, my brother, my grandmother, and the cats. Even though they can easily afford a housekeeper, Gram runs the house and fixes all our meals while Mom and Dad work and travel. Gram does it because she loves it, and I can't knock that. The trouble is that she's the world's worst cook. Yuck. Whenever I complain to my mother, she begs, "Humor her, dear. She means well." Jonathan and I try hard, but when we're alone and Gram has her back turned, we roll our eyes at each other, puff out our cheeks, and pretend to vomit all over the table. It's the only time we really get along. Cindy and Jasper, our oversized ginger-colored cats, who are Gram's only fans, are usually waiting silently under the table to devour her latest masterpiece. Together, fools that they are, they weigh nearly as much as Jonathan, who's in the fourth grade.

But the cats didn't turn into lead balloons overnight; it's been happening ever since I can remember. No, lately it's people like Mr. Guild and things at school that are out of control. Just like the concerts, I used to like school. Elementary school was fun, and so was junior high. But freshman year at North Hollow High was a disaster. Suddenly, people seemed to care that I was the daughter of West and Lane. Some of them would back away, or, more horrible, they would want something from me. Mr. Rush, my English teacher, was the worst.

Last year I spent all of my free time with Jennifer, my best friend since the first grade. Together, we did all of our homework, giggled over John Fox, an adorable boy in social studies class, and avoided the hundreds of strangers that filled North Hollow High.

But in July, just before my parents' big annual New York concert, Jennifer and her family had moved away to Washington. I was devastated. How would I live without Jennifer? I knew practically no one at school, and though I was sure there were plenty of people who would like to be friendly with me for the status of knowing the daughter of West and Lane, how would I ever meet anyone who would like me for myself?

Since she had moved, Jen and I had talked on the phone and even written a few letters to each other, but it just wasn't the same. It wasn't like having a friend nearby that you could always depend on.

Then a couple of days after Mom and Dad's big New York concert, I met my neighbor Susan for the first time.

"I feel a little embarrassed," she told me when I answered the front door that morning and then went on in a rush, "But we live next door, and we have some unexpected guests. I was in the middle of making lemonade when I realized I was low on sugar. Would you mind?" The short, pretty stranger with close-cut blond curls held out a measuring cup.

"Don't be silly," I told her, "Come into the kitchen. If we have any, you're welcome to it." Gram's sugar canister was well stocked, and I was able to fill the measuring cup. "By the way, I'm Barbara Lane," I told her.

"I'm sorry." She looked embarrassed. "I'm Susan Hanover, and I'm glad to meet you. We moved in last January. It's weird that we've never met before. Do you go to North Hollow High?"

"Yes, I'll be a sophomore," I said.

"Oh. I'll be a junior. Well, I've really got to run. It's my father's sister and her new husband who have dropped in. My mother's fit to be tied," she confided in a whisper as she slipped out the door. "Thanks a million."

Later that afternoon, when she thoughtfully brought us a pitcher of her potent lemonade (such a treat after Gram's lemon-scented sugar water), I invited her to cool off in our pool. My folks had gone off to L.A. to work just after their concert, and though there were moments when I really missed them, at that instant it was a relief to know they weren't around. Mom, especially, has a way of dominating any conversation. It was going to be hard enough talking to a stranger without Mom's well-meaning but overbearing presence.

Although Susan declined my offer, over the next few weeks, of a swim, we managed to go to the movies together a couple of steamy afternoons, play Spite and Malice during the evenings in our air-conditioned den, and collaborate on several fresh fruit salad lunches in the Hanover's blue-and-white kitchen. Finding Susan open and cheerful and not particularly interested in the comings and goings of my famous parents, I was delighted to discover that I was, after all, capable of talking to someone other than Jennifer.

By the time the first day of school rolled around, I was feeling so good that when Gram called "Breakfast!" I went downstairs cheerfully. In my mind, I was already there, meeting new kids, having a new English teacher, and maybe even finding the boy of my dreams.

I nibbled at my French toast, hardly minding its soggy texture, while Gram instructed Jonathan in the use of maple syrup. "Sweetheart, try to pour a little more slowly next time. It comes all the way from Vermont, and we don't want to waste a drop." Unimpressed, Jonathan made no comment. He was too busy refitting the retro rockets into the Star Wars rocket launcher and licking his sticky fingers.

Pushing myself away from the table after only a few bites, I headed for the kitchen sink to rinse my own sticky fingers. "How will you ever have enough energy for the morning on what you've eaten?" Gram objected, surveying the toast and three-quarters-full glass of milk.

"I'll make it," I promised. "It's just that my stomach is a bit unsettled, first day of school and all." My stomach felt like the inside of a monkey house at playtime.

"Peppermint tea will do the trick," announced Gram as she lit the flame under the kettle.

"Thanks, but I can't wait," I yelled over my shoulder as I grabbed for my bag and notebook and escaped out the door. "Bye, you guys." Jonathan was still flying missiles over his plate, his hands and forearms dappled with syrup.

Outside, the morning was sunny, a breeze cooling the late summer air, and there was no one on the sidewalk. As I started to walk toward school, trying to will my stomach to relax, I heard someone run up behind me. It was Susan. "Wait up," she panted.

"I didn't know if you had gone, or if I should stop at the house," I told her. Susan's mother worked late at night on her fabric designs and slept most mornings.

"It's just as well you didn't," she confirmed. "The bell might have awakened Mom."

Though in the few weeks we had known each other, we had come to like each other a lot, I knew that in school Susan had her own special group of friends. She seemed relaxed and undaunted this morning, I noticed, probably because this year wouldn't be much different for her than last.

"How are you doing?" she asked.

"I'm not sure. It's going to be weird without Jennifer."

"I know," she commiserated. "When we moved here in January, I didn't know a soul. It was really scary. But it turned out fine. Wait and see. You'll meet other kids in no time. Think positive."

"Part of me knows you're right. And besides, even if I miss my old pal Jen, I know I won't miss my old English teacher. I really am excited about having someone new. Maybe I'll get Davis or Stein. Even Langhorn wouldn't be so bad. Anything will be an improvement over Rush."

Susan was shaking her head. "I had Rush for English last year, and he wasn't the greatest, but, Barb, he wasn't that bad either, and he is really cute."

Shivering involuntarily, I had to concede this last comment. "Did he have any pets when you had him? Think."

Susan was silent for a moment. "Yes, I think he might have."

"And did he have any pet hates?" I persisted.

"I guess so. Oh, yeh, I do remember one boy, Ronnie something-or-other."

"Well, I was one of them last year, and it was hideous."

"How come? Did you goof off a lot or something?"

I had never told Susan the whole story. It was too painful. The only one who knew what really had happened was Jennifer, and though she thought my solution was crazy, it was my own private battle, and not even Jennifer could convince me to change my mind. "I can't go into it right now," I explained, shaking my head, and Susan seemed satisfied to let the subject drop. We walked on in silence, and I thought about Mr. Rush and what it was I couldn't bring myself to talk about.

At the beginning of freshman year, he had gone out of his way to be nice to me, spending time helping me with compositions and praising me in front of the class—not that I had asked for or expected any special attention.

One day he asked me to come back eighth period to discuss my latest essay. When he had finished complimenting me, he began talking about himself. Mr. Rush, it seemed, was an unpublished songwriter. "And I'm looking forward to meeting your folks one of these days," he told me.

I found myself having similar conversations with him over the next few weeks, but it wasn't until he added, "having a song sung by the great West and Lane is a sure way to have a smash," that I was hit with the awful truth. Furious, disappointed, mortified, and not sure what to do, there was one thing I knew for certain. If Mr. Rush was being nice to me because he expected a favor in return, I didn't want any part of it. I just wanted to be another student in his class.

Fending off several more outright requests, I finally told him, "I hardly ever talk to them about their work. Please understand that even though they are my parents, there are lots of things I don't know about them and lots of things I don't want to know. I'm afraid I can't help you."

Although I was able to escape from this confrontation without further comment, the issue was far from closed. A few weeks went by, and I made no attempt to accommodate Mr. Rush. Then one day, though I had continued to do my work diligently, as I had always done, my grades plummeted, and I found myself being singled out in class for doing sloppy work. Whereas I could see that Mr. Rush might once have been inflating my grades to win my favors, I knew that he was now downgrading me to win my compliance. Neither felt right, and though the low grades weren't nearly as painful as he might have wished, the out and out harassment was unendurable.

I went to my guidance counselor to ask for a section change, but beyond a mild "personality conflict," I couldn't bring myself to describe the problem in any more detail. It was just too awful. As a result, Mrs. Squire advised me to "hang in and work harder," offering to set me up with a tutor to help bolster my grades. I guess mind reading isn't one of her specialties. I cut English last year as much as I dared, avoiding all of my classmates except for Jennifer.

Near the end of the year, Mr. Rush made an announcement to the class that sent my heart lurching. "I'm sending around a sheet of paper," he told the class. "Sign it if you'd like to be recommended for the sophomore journalism class and a chance to write for the paper. Your grades have to be B or better, so don't even bother to sign up if you know they're lower. Anyone in doubt can ask me if they're eligible." I felt sure he was glaring at me. I knew beyond a doubt that I wouldn't qualify, and it killed me. Could he know how I felt?

I'm proud to say that never once that year did I consider complaining to my parents or giving in to Rush as Jennifer had urged. As a matter of principle, it was more important to stand up for my right to be myself.

I squeaked by freshman English with a C- and considered myself lucky. Although my mother raised an eyebrow when she saw my grade, she only said, "English was never my favorite subject either." The trouble was it *had* been my favorite subject. Both my seventh- and eighth-grade teachers had encouraged my passion for reading and writing. I had loved being on the junior high paper.

Now, as Susan and I neared school and the sidewalks were filling up with students, the streets with yellow buses, I was looking forward to a fresh start.

Susan greeted two of her friends whom she introduced to me as Christine and Joy. Acknowledging each other politely, we fell in step together as we walked up the granite steps, through the columned portico, and into the echoing main lobby of North Hollow High. Susan and Christine were deep in conversation, and I found myself talking to Joy above the roar of the monstrous room.

"Are you new here?" Joy wanted to know. "I've never seen you before."

"No," I told her, "but I'm a sophomore."

"Oh," Joy seemed to be digesting this. "I'm a junior. Susan, Chris, and I are in the math club together. Are you thinking of joining. Sophomores are welcome, you know."

Although I knew the math club wasn't for me, I didn't have time to answer. It was 8:27; there were three minutes to find homeroom.

"Barb, look for us at lunch," Susan called over. Smiling at her thoughtfulness, I waved and took off down the hall. This was what I had been waiting for all summer, a second chance.

I headed up the stairs, but as it turned out, it wasn't so easy to get where I was going. The whole world had waited until the last moment and was now in a hurry to reach homeroom, too. Suddenly, the crowd turned into a stampeding herd of animals, and I found myself being bounced back and forth between shoulders, elbows, and notebooks as hundreds of us tried to climb the stairs in a single wave.

I looked around, panic rising in me, trying to understand what was happening. A few raucous kids were pushing and laughing, propelling the rest of us forward. We were stumbling and tripping over the steps and each other, and a lot of kids were getting really mad.

Then, in the middle of the chaos, a rich masculine voice next to me shouted out, "Hey, you guys, take it easy," and I looked up to see this tall guy with dark hair and a gorgeous face standing just to my left. "Easy, easy," he continued, his voice miraculously cutting through the madness, turning the mounting wave of hysteria back into a tame little ripple.

I reached the top of the stairs and walked down

the comparatively peaceful hall, trying to keep my eye on the commanding stranger, but he had vanished into the crowd. What a knockout, I thought to myself; maybe he'll turn up in one of my classes.

Homeroom was half filled with students, some sitting at desks, others wandering impatiently. I sat down at a desk and began to look around while more students trickled in. The gorgeous stranger from the stairs was missing, a great disappointment.

Within a few seconds a small, neat woman came into the room and wrote on the board, Homeroom 328 S. Then she sat behind the big desk and waited for the bell to ring. "Class, I'm Anne Ricciardi," she told the quieted group. "Check your sheets to make sure you are in the right homeroom. Since we have a lot to do in our ten minutes together, we'll have to work quickly." She spoke in a friendly but efficient voice. "You've gotten your schedule sheets, I assume, or you wouldn't be here. I've got your class cards, teacher assignments, and locker numbers. She indicated a stack of yellowish cards that she had placed on the desk in front of her. "Check to be sure you have eight cards in your pile. Anyone whose name I don't call, see me when the bell rings. I'm going to work quickly, so please do your best to pick up your cards and return to your seats in a thoughtful, orderly fashion. Anderson, Centalla, Copeland . . ." She began calling off names in groups of three, and when she got to "Kalt, Lambert, Lane," I practically ran up to retrieve my stack, murmuring "excuse me" as I bumped into a returning student.

My excitement was nearly out of control as I sat down at my desk and pulled the rubber band from my pile of cards. Was it silly, I wondered, that my hands were trembling?

Anne Ricciardi's voice was swirling around the room, and bodies were coming and going through the aisles. But I had stopped noticing everything around me. Turning to my sixth period class card to see who I had gotten for English, the shock was so overwhelming that everything else had faded away. "This must be a mistake," I screamed inside my head. "How could this be true!" I clutched at my desk as my whole body tensed. Printed in delicate computer letters on my rectangular punch card was the name RUSH.

2

The bell rang, and I wandered toward study hall, my head in a fog. When I had first gotten my schedule sheet in the mail, I had been glad to have study hall first thing in the morning, a definite improvement over freshman year when gym had been my first-period class.

Now I wasn't so sure. The day had gotten off to such a bad start that I was horrified by the idea of spending forty minutes in silent contemplation.

Study hall was a massive room filled with over a hundred battered desks and attached chairs set in neat rows. At the front was a raised platform, furnished with a huge desk from which Mrs. Bradshaw imposed her rule of deadly silence.

I sat down at a desk near the windows on the left side of the room, far away from where I had sat last year. The bell rang, and Mrs. Bradshaw began speaking in her familiar, nearly hysterical voice. "People, take your seats immediately. This is a study hall, not Grand Central Station." A large woman with ruddy face and short mousy hair, she was standing on the platform, arms out, hands motioning downward.

"You have exactly thirty seconds to find your seats," she was telling the still buzzing group, "and the places you take will be yours for the rest of the year." Then each student had to give his or her name for Mrs. Bradshaw's seating chart and hand in his or her computer card. "Keep yourselves busy for the rest of the period. Let's not get off to a bad start. Anyone caught talking to a neighbor will have to answer the consequences."

As she rattled on about the rules and regulations of study hall, I sat at my desk and stared straight ahead, vaguely aware of the students who had filled in the places around me. I knew I would probably feel better if I could write a letter to Jennifer, but I couldn't will myself to take out a pen or even open my notebook. When I felt a gentle brushing against my ankle, I turned to look down, somehow expecting to see Jasper, Gram's cat.

Instead, I saw a lanky boy with dark, tangled hair, shyly grinning up at me. He was wearing jeans that were so worn, they were almost white, a short-sleeved rugby shirt, and scruffy suede running shoes. He had a folded piece of unlined notebook paper in his hand, which he held near the floor; although his posture was purposefully ambiguous and meant to make him look as if he were picking up a piece of paper he had dropped, I knew by the look on his face that the sheet was meant for me. First glancing up at Mrs. Bradshaw, who appeared to be immersed in entering names in her roll book, I bent over and picked up the paper. The boy, who was already sitting upright at his desk, I had instantly recognized as Sandy Moore. He had been in my freshman English class, and his experience with Rush, I knew, had probably been almost as painful as my own.

Sandy was the class doodler. His light blue cloth-covered notebook had been famous for being covered with offbeat, intricate drawings of cars, buildings, and an occasional portrait. In addition to the notebook, I also remembered clearly the drawing he had done last year of Mr. Rush. Filling a sheet of notebook paper with delicate crosshatches, Sandy had pictured the well-dressed Mr. Rush with a bulbously large head, shark-like teeth, and giant hands. Although Sandy had kept Rush's athletic body tiny, he had drawn the hands in the same elephantine proportions as the head. To me, the portrait had been startlingly accurate.

How Sandy's caricature ended up on Rush's desk, I never knew. Sandy showed his drawing to a neighbor, who found it so amusing that he or she passed it on. I had always felt awful knowing that I had unwittingly contributed to Sandy's downfall. The portrait had been passed from Marie Gilbert, who sat behind me. Enjoying it, I thoughtlessly passed it forward to Todd Seigal. Did some jerk pass it to Rush, or did he discover it weaving its way through class? I couldn't remember. No matter what happened, Rush did see it, and from then on, Sandy's life in freshman English was hell.

Although we had both been victims of Rush's enduring anger, we had never gotten together to discuss our common problem. Instead, as soon as the bell had rung, we each ran out, tails between our legs. Now we were to be study hall neighbors, and Sandy was starting the year with a note whose contents I wondered about. I also wondered whether picking it up and reading it was an invitation for trouble. But Bradshaw, immersed in work, seemed not to notice. What harm could there be in reading a note?

Carefully unfolding the paper, I discovered a sprawling drawing Sandy had done with a fine-lined black pen in his own humorous style. He had sketched the study hall with Mrs. Bradshaw huddled over her desk in demonic concentration. At the other desks, students were at work in a variety of positions. Over Mrs. Bradshaw's head and those of many of the students were thought-balloons, comic book style. Mrs. Bradshaw's balloon was filled with a figure lighting a bundle of dynamite sticks under an abbreviated sketch of what could only be North Hollow High. The students' balloons were filled with visions of sailboats, and movie theaters. One student was shown as merely a lump in bed under a polka-dot cover. I looked for and found that Sandy had left my thought-balloon empty. Sandy's self-portrait, just next to the drawing of me, had a thought-balloon that was filled with a rocket ship, traveling through outer space.

Grinning in appreciation, I looked toward Sandy, who had turned over his hand and raised his eyebrows, silently requesting me to fill in my own balloon. I dove into my bag, ennui forgotten, and pulled out my pen, wondering what to draw. I thought for a few minutes and got to work on two palm trees with a hammock slung between them and a primitively drawn figure lying peacefully in it. Hoping to show that I wished I were far out at sea, I drew a tiny mound under the trees and surrounded it with wavy ripples of water.

Then, out of a driving impulse to somehow test this stranger, up in a corner of the paper I wrote, "Didn't you have enough drawing last year in English class?" After checking to see that Bradshaw was still occupied, I silently passed the note back to Sandy.

"Never too much," Sandy wrote under my question, slipping the paper deftly back on my desk. "It's my responsibility to record for posterity what happens at North Hollow. Neither rain, nor sleet, nor threat of Bradshaw will keep this artist from his appointed rounds." It was a lighthearted reply, inviting no particular response, but after a moment of hesitation, I recklessly pushed on with my urge to communicate.

"You can joke," I complained, "but I've struck out for the second year in a row. Guess whom I've got for English?"

"Donelly?" was Sandy's written reply. Donelly was reputed to be a witch.

"Worse," I answered, having to fit my words around the thought-balloon that was filled with the sleeping lump. RUSH, I wrote in dark letters. By now, after checking on Bradshaw, we were merely handing our correspondence back and forth to each other.

I held up the yellow card for him to see across the aisle.

"It has to be a mistake," he answered back, turning the paper sideways to fit his latest comment into a blank space between the drawings. "Who's your counselor?"

"Squire."

"Mine, too. She's okay. Why don't you ask her for a section change?" he answered. "There must be some kind of law to protect people from having Rush two years in a row."

Mrs. Bradshaw was getting up from her desk and moving toward the side of the room where we were sitting. In a panic, I tucked the note into the back of my looseleaf and began scribbling on a blank page, hoping to look like I was immersed in some worthwhile project.

To my relief, I saw that Mrs. Bradshaw was only beginning to open windows. With the morning sun pouring through them, the room had gotten stiflingly hot. The first two windows, at the back of the room, seemed to open easily, but the third, nearer to us, wasn't going to budge. As Mrs. Bradshaw continued to struggle with it, Sandy got up from his seat. "May I help you?" he offered politely. I couldn't remember hearing his voice before, although I must have sometime last year, and I was surprised by its pleasant tone.

What a fool, I thought, Bradshaw's going to jump right down his throat. But Bradshaw surprised me.

"Thank you, young man," she told Sandy, "I would appreciate some assistance, and if all else fails, you can summon the custodian."

Sandy, his long arms more muscular than I would have imagined, opened the windows easily.

Mrs. Bradshaw blustered an uncharacteristic thank you, and Sandy sat down at his desk, a suspiciously wide grin spreading across his face.

He drew a quick sketch of himself with angel wings
and a halo, which he cautiously flashed at me when
Bradshaw's attention was elsewhere. I hoped to
make some appropriate comment in return. But
while I was considering what to say, the bell rang
and Sandy was gone. Boy, that's fast, I thought; he
really does have wings. And with that, all thoughts
of Sandy flew from my mind.

Geometry and history were painless. Although
Mr. Hazeltine seemed a shade too serious, Mrs.
Harris, who was about a hundred years old, was such
a great storyteller that after a few minutes I forgot
where I was and got lost in adventures in the
mountains of Peru. As soon as the bell rang, her
spell was broken, and I dashed down to Mrs.
Squire's office.

Somehow, I knew it was going to be hopeless, and
after fifteen minutes of waiting, Mrs. Squire confirmed my fears. "You see," I had explained to her,
"I've got Mr. Rush again for English. I had him last
year and we . . . er . . . didn't get along very well.
Isn't there some way I could get a section change?"

"Yes, I do remember your problems with him,"
Mrs. Squire answered, "and ordinarily you shouldn't
be having the same teacher two years in a row." An
attractive woman in her sixties, she had a harried
look on her face. Her desk was covered with an
avalanche of papers. "Let me look, Barbara. That
was sixth period, you said, with lunch fifth." She was
flipping through her master schedule list. "Oh dear,
there don't seem to be any other sophomore sections
those periods. How odd. I don't think there's a thing
I can do." Her voice was regretful.

"Mrs. Squire, I'd do anything at all to get someone else, even if it meant switching gym to first period."

"I understand, but as you can see, we're in a terrible jam here. Scheduling was supposed to be made foolproof by the fancy new computer the district bought, but the darn thing seems to have gotten everything wrong, and the trouble started somewhere back in July when no one was here to stop it. I'd say you were pretty lucky to have all your basic classes straight at all. I'm getting kids with two and three classes scheduled into the same time slot or biology twice in one day and no math, if you can imagine that. But I'll see what I can do," she promised. "Honestly, though, we're in such a tangle here that I don't know which way is up."

Although I believed she would try, it didn't lessen the frustration I felt at the moment, and I was close to tears as I left her office. The line to see Mrs. Squire, which had grown to fifteen or twenty people, was snaking through the outer office and into the hall.

With only a few minutes left until the end of fifth period, I knew I wouldn't have time for lunch. Besides, knowing Rush's class was coming up next, who could eat! Trudging up the three flights of stairs to Rush's classroom, I wondered if I should skip this first class altogether and appeal to my parents for help. One call to Mr. Hollingsworth, the principal, would be enough to end my misery. But no, I decided. After resisting this temptation all last year, why should I give in to it now? It was more important to solve this problem myself and not depend on being the daughter of the famous couple West and Lane.

Am I crazy? I wondered. This is getting out of control. Taking a desk at the back of the room, I waited for Rush to arrive. My devastating stranger from the stairs that morning still hadn't appeared. I did, however, recognize a few of the other kids from last year, and one girl, Jane Hartley, who had been in last year's French class, gave me a big smile before taking one of the last empty seats in the room, several rows in front of me.

Rush arrived seconds before the bell rang and put a pile of his books on the front desk. Looking natty in his corduroy sport jacket, with leather elbow patches and blue button-down shirt, his blond hair freshly trimmed, he introduced himself to the quieted group. I barely listened as he asked for class cards and went on to describe the year ahead. Instead, I stared at him as if I might discern some important transformation in his personality. What did I see? It was the same pretty tanned face with the upturned nose and pale blue eyes looking just as grotesquely babyish to me as it had last year.

I forced my mind back into focus in time to take notes on the reading assignments for the coming week. Then he handed out battered paperback copies of *To Kill a Mockingbird,* and the class took turns reading aloud. When it was my turn, he acknowledged me with the same impersonal nod he had given the other students, and I went through my passage, keeping my voice well modulated, a struggle I hoped no one would detect.

When the bell finally rang, I flew out of the

classroom, camouflaged in a mob of students. I was practically the first person in French class, and when Jane Hartley walked in, a few minutes later, she took the empty chair on my right.

We gave each other a smile and sat up straight as a tall dark-haired woman in her mid-thirties came into the room, a somber expression on her face. I was afraid we were in for a bad year.

"Soyez les bienvenus! Je m'appelle Mademoiselle Moran," she began slowly in a soft cultured French accent, her face lighting up. *"Je suis contente de vous revoir en classe."*

I leaned forward in concentration, fascinated. There was a lot Mlle. Moran was saying that went right past me, but after a few minutes, I was delighted to discover that some of the meaning was filtering through. So first year French hadn't been in vain!

After school that afternoon, when the little homework I had was done, I dropped by to see Susan, but her sister told me she had gone shopping. So, instead, I went home and started a letter to Jennifer, telling her the whole horrible story to date and promising to keep her posted on all the new developments. Although I had considered calling Jennifer on the phone, getting it all down on paper seemed as though it would be more satisfying, and it was.

The next morning, I walked to school again with Susan.

"Where were you yesterday? We looked for you at lunch," she told me. I told her about my scheduling disaster.

"So now what?" she wanted to know.

"I'm not sure."

"Why don't you get your mother to pressure Hollingsworth a little? It would be a cinch."

I shook my head. "No, that would be too easy. I fought that battle last year, and I'm not about to give in now."

"You're nuts," said Susan with a disgusted shrug, and she knew enough to let the subject drop.

In study hall I had planned to read more of *To Kill a Mockingbird*, which I really liked, but before I could read more than a dozen pages, Sandy slipped a note onto my desk. "Did you see Squire?" he had printed.

"I have been a victim of the supposedly foolproof new computer," I answered back.

Sandy read my note and shook his head, then set to work on another piece of paper. Whatever it was, I could see it was going to be a few minutes in the making, so I turned back to my book, re-reading page twelve for the third time that morning. While Sandy's pen scratched furiously, I actually read a few more pages before being presented with an elaborate drawing, and it was worth the wait. He had created a giant computer. Covered with buttons and jewels, eight or ten arms with gloved hands came out from the sides and circled around to the front to grip a small figure. Although only my face and feet stuck out, I could tell it was me. In the corner was a three-dimensional-looking drawing of an army medal, complete with ribbon, which read, "Presented in Recognition of Valor Shown in the Battle Against the District II Computer."

"Thanks," I told him on a small scrap of paper, "I needed that." Sandy tipped his hand to me and went back to work on an elaborate car that he had begun to draw on the cover of his new denim notebook. Tucking his sketch into a manila folder at the back of my own looseleaf, I opened *To Kill a Mockingbird* again. I stared at the pages as if I were concentrating, but now my will to read was gone. Instead, I let my eyes shift slightly so I could surreptitiously study Sandy.

His was the garbage can look: stringy and uncombed hair, stretched out navy blue T-shirt, and holey jeans. But it wasn't his choice of clothing or lack of grooming that put me off; it was his single-minded devotion to his drawing. With his thick hair hanging down, obscuring his face, and his lean body crouched over his desk, here, I knew, was no football hero or student leader type.

Suddenly, I remembered a rating system Jennifer and I had invented last year. It was a silly scale, I know, but it had worked for us. North Hollow High, built on five levels, had been the inspiration. The highest score was "third floor;" the lowest, "subbasement;" with "basement," "main," and "second" in between.

John Fox, though neither of us had ever spoken to him, had been the one person in our third-floor category. He was great looking, and Jennifer had been madly in love with him. I felt sure that the gorgeous guy I had seen in the hall yesterday, who had been drifting in and out of my thoughts since then, would deserve a place in the third-floor category, and I was planning to write a long letter to Jennifer to tell her all about him.

Jennifer would have thrown grubby Sandy instantly into the subbasement. I was thinking basement might be more accurate. But even this seemed unfair. I had hardly spoken to Sandy directly, and yet I felt we had established some form of communication. Already, he was more of a real person than our idol John Fox had been. The concept of the rating scale, so infallible last year, was giving me trouble. I watched Sandy out of the corner of my eye for as long as I dared before I made up my mind. No, the scale was okay. It was Sandy. He was a real weirdo.

3

By the third week of school I was really down in the dumps. My folks still hadn't gotten back from their latest business trip, and school was a bummer. The person I missed the most, though, was Jennifer, and I had been spending a lot of time writing her letters. The first one turned out to be twenty-two pages long, and I had to buy a special manila envelope to mail it in.

Jennifer wrote me back a pretty long letter. It was seven pages, but her handwriting is big. I sent her another one, eighteen pages long, that she didn't answer at all. Finally, I got tired of waiting, so I called Jennifer on the phone, but she was too busy studying for a bio quiz to spend time talking. Crummy as it made me feel, I had to face facts. Things between me and Jennifer just weren't ever going to be the same.

Meantime, at school, Susan had been inviting me

to sit with her and her friends during lunch, and while they were friendly enough toward me, they became so engrossed in things—like new ways to solve Rubik's Cube—that it was sometimes easier for me to sit on the lawn and eat lunch by myself than pretend to be involved.

One morning, on our way to school, I was feeling especially dragged out, when Susan nailed me. "Okay," she challenged in a determined voice that was one of her best assets, "are you going to get off your behind before it's too late, or what?" She was eyeing me up and down.

"I'm not sure what you mean," I stalled.

"Come off it, you're not the perky Barbara Lane I met last summer, fun to be with, smiling, happy. You're becoming a real drag. What's going on here?"

"Nothing. This is the real me."

"Give me a break. You're even dressing different-ly. Excuse me, but I can't help noticing how elegant you look."

Since I was wearing an ancient, stained thermal-underwear shirt, filthy jeans, and my hair was a mess, I couldn't continue to deny her accusations. I finally admitted, "If you really want to know, school is turning out to be a bomb, even worse than last year, if that's possible."

"Is it Rush?" she asked.

"No, I don't think so; he's pretty much leaving me alone so far. It's just general sick city, if you know what I mean." There was a lot I couldn't put into words, and my voice was quavering.

"Barbara, you need some new friends." Her voice had become sympathetic.

"But I have friends. You and Chris have been terrific," I sniffed.

"That's not what I mean. Math club, chess, and Rubik's Cube are not for you; it doesn't take much to see that. You need other stuff. Why don't you join intramurals?"

"Yuck. I hate volleyball."

"Glee club."

"Are you kidding?"

"Well, I figured, because of your parents and all—"

"You figured wrong. I'd rather wash dishes in the cafeteria." I'm happy to say that in my vehemence against sports and singing, I had managed to regain my composure.

We walked in silence for part of the block. "I would like to be on the *Clarion*," I announced.

"The school paper? That's a great idea. So what's the big deal?"

"Well, you have to be in journalism class."

"So?"

"So you need a B in English to get in, and Rush gave me a C last year. Of course, I didn't deserve it."

"Oh, Lord." Susan rolled her eyes at me. "That can't be the only way to get on the paper."

"It's the only way I know of to get on the writing staff. Maybe I'll do better in Rush's class this year, and I'll make junior journalism."

"Yeh, but can you wait that long? It looks to me like you're about to climb under a rock and die."

"I look that bad?" I asked, and received a look of pure exasperation.

Susan may have felt as though she were beating me over the head with a sledge hammer, but it was the sort of gentle little push I needed to get my mind racing. I would volunteer for the school paper, I decided in homeroom. I would sweep floors and sharpen pencils, if need be, until I got my first break.

Later in study hall, as my mind raced, I noticed Sandy sketching in a little black covered book, and I was pretty sure he was drawing me! What should I do? I wondered. Should I object? Should I cooperate? Should I pretend I didn't know what he was doing?

Instead, I fell into a reverie. Ninth period, I would go to the newspaper office and volunteer to count paper clips. The decision made, I looked over to Sandy, who was twiddling his pencil rapidly in the air between two fingers.

"Were you drawing me?" I wrote on a scrap of paper from my looseleaf, then I stealthily plunked it onto his desk. He held the sketch down by his side for me to see. I was used to Sandy's lighthearted cartoons, so this drawing was a surprise. Although I wouldn't have known it was me, as the hand supporting my head was obscuring my face, the drawing was impressively realistic.

"You're really good," I told him in a note.

"Thanks," he wrote underneath, and I think he blushed.

"Do you do anything with your drawings?" I wrote.

"Like what?"

"I don't know. Hang them up?"

"No, I just do them."

"Do you ever do any for the *Clarion?*" I braved, my handwriting getting smaller as room on the scrap paper ran out.

"That scandal sheet! No, if anywhere, I'd like to sell drawings to the *New Yorker.*" He had turned the paper over and was using sloppy script, which was unusual for Sandy, who mostly printed neatly.

"Wow. Did you ever try?"

"Are you kidding? Have you ever noticed all the drawings they print by high school kids?"

"Well, you do have to start somewhere, so why not at North Hollow?" There was absolutely no room left on the scrap paper we had been using, and I wondered if Sandy would continue this fascinating correspondence. I was pleased to see him pull a sheet of paper from his notebook and get to work on a quick drawing. It took a few minutes, and when it was done he slipped it on my desk. "The Universe according to Sandy Moore," it said. The paper was divided by arcing lines that made a giant rainbow, on the top of which was the *New Yorker* and the *New York Times,* and below it was *Playboy.* In the lowest arc was the *Enquirer,* the *National Star* and North Hollow High *Clarion.* I had seen the *Star* and *Enquirer* in the supermarket, and while I had never bought either, I knew they were pretty gross. I had to laugh at his drawing. Sandy was into rating systems, too!

So Sandy wasn't interested in the *Clarion.* Big deal. What did it matter to me? In my estimation, the school paper was a fine place to start.

I sat through the day dying for the arrival of ninth period, when I figured someone was sure to be downstairs in the newspaper office. Whoever it was, I was determined to talk to someone.

As Jennifer and I had discovered last year, the basement, with its damp, gloomy hallways and painted cement floor, was only slightly better than the sub-basement, which was absolutely creepy. It always seemed chilly down there, and I shivered as I passed the doors to the chess club and the math club, finally arriving at the *Clarion* office. The doors were made of dark heavy wood with chipped gold numbers that marked each room.

I knew it was the right office because taped on the door there was an outdated June paper with a typed list of the new fall staff posted just below. Going down the list of names, I discovered that they were all strange to me. I reached for the battered doorknob as I was finishing the list but stopped myself before I could push open the door. Every curse word I knew went through my mind. Guess who was the faculty advisor. It pains me to even say the name: Mr. Rush!

I turned around and headed up the stairs and out the front door of North Hollow High. That was it. I was never going back. My parents had often offered to send me to private school, and though I had repeatedly refused, now it seemed like a great idea.

I steamed all the way home and marched in the front door. Gram was working on a crossword puzzle, which she put down long enough to tempt me with chocolate chip cookies and milk. Waving cryptically, I ran past her, went up to my room, and threw myself down on the bed. I'm not sure how long I lay there, but when the phone rang and

Jonathan yelled that it was Susan, I didn't even have the energy to say I would call back. I let them think I was sleeping.

Eventually, Gram called me for dinner, and I dragged myself off the bed and downstairs. It was fish sticks, and even the bought ones are better.

"When are Mom and Dad getting back?" I asked her. Lately I had found it easier not to keep track of their schedule. When they got home, they would be home, and I had for the most part learned to run my life without them.

"They should be back sometime Monday," Gram said.

"Are they in Los Angeles?"

"I should imagine so. They were hoping to sign that new record deal and start recording."

"I'm going to call them tonight," I announced. "Do either of you want to say hello?" Jonathan had turned his fish sticks into little bombs, which he was launching over the edge of the table to Jasper.

"Yes, I could ask your mother what she wants to do about the dry cleaner," she told me. "They still can't find your father's suede jacket." Then turning, she said with a gush, "Oh Jonathan, you've finished all your fish, like a good boy. Would you like some more?"

"No thanks," he answered politely. On his face was a look of pure horror.

I was figuring in my head the time in California. It was 6:30 P.M. in New York. That would be 3:30 A.M. in Los Angeles.

"Call the studio first, and if they're not there leave a message. You might want to wait till about 10, our time, to try the hotel." Gram advised.

"Okay, I'm calling from my room. I'll let you know when I'm done." Gulping down the last of my brussels sprouts, I grabbed the small spiral-backed phone book and ran up the stairs two at a time. "I want to talk," Jonathan yelled.

I put through a person-to-person call to my mother at the studio, and it was a relief to finally hear her voice. "Sweetheart, how are you. Is everything all right?" She sounded really happy to hear from me. "How are Jonathan and Gram?" We talked a little about familiar things, and finally I built up my courage.

"Mom, remember last year when you suggested Lloyd's school, and I kept saying North Hollow's good enough?"

"Yes."

"Well, school is horrible this year, and I really want to change." She was silent for a moment.

"That's fine, dear, if that's what you want. We'll check into it first thing Tuesday morning."

"Great Mom, thanks."

"But, sweetie, promise me one thing."

"Sure, anything."

"Keep going to your classes until then and take any tests that you have coming up. You may hate Lloyd's, so don't burn your bridges just yet. Huh, sweetie?"

"Mom, I'll be good, I promise."

"Great. Do you want to say hi to Dad?"

"Sure, and Gram wants to talk when we're done; so does Jon." I said a quick hello to my father and then turned the phone over to my grandmother. Good. That was settled. I would leave North Hollow High and Mr. Rush behind. Maybe all those snobby kids in private school wouldn't be so bad after all.

The day after I spoke to my mother was Friday, and I woke up feeling great. I had decided not to spill my big news to Susan about changing schools. Somehow, I thought I might hurt her feelings. But I spent the day mentally saying goodbye to all my teachers. I even gave Rush a big fat smirk.

It's funny how things happen when you least expect them, because suddenly there was that gorgeous guy I had been dreaming about ever since I had seen him on the stairs that first day of school! He was sitting on the stage during weekly assembly with two other kids who were also running for student council president.

"Hi, I'm Tim Halpern," he told the entire school, with a voice that was strong and relaxed, just as I had remembered it. "For those of you who don't know me, I'm captain of the basketball team this year." A large contingent near the front of the auditorium started to cheer. "North Hollow's a great place, and what makes it so great are the after-school activities. Not only are our sports teams the best, but so is our band, our debating society, and even our glee club. The trouble is that this year, more than ever, we need to raise our own money for new equipment, traveling expenses, and stuff like that. As student council president, I plan to launch the most fun, most profitable fund-raising drive ever." He began to elaborate on an impressive plan, which I listened to without breathing. His voice was deep and rich, and he spoke to the entire group as if he were speaking to his best friend. The previous speakers had been a very serious girl named Linda Mullen and a boy named Brian Jacoby, whose stuttering had been painful to hear. I had squirmed in my seat while he spoke, praying that his speech would be over quickly. Someone a few rows behind me snickered.

No one was snickering at Tim, I noticed. He was wearing a crisp, madras shirt, khaki slacks that fit just right, and polished loafers. I couldn't see that far, but I was willing to bet there were pennies in his shoes.

He was tall, as one would expect of a basketball player, but he was unusually muscular. Again, I remembered that rating scale Jennifer and I had used so mercilessly to judge the boys in school. When I had seen Tim that first day of school, I had an inkling that he would go up in the third-floor category with John Fox. Actually, it was Jennifer who had put John up there, while I had felt there was still room at the top.

An inner voice told me that the scale was really stupid. After all, how could it work if it meant putting a talented person like that Sandy Moore in the basement with all the rest of the creeps? Sandy might be a weirdo, but he was my friend, sort of. But what did it matter now, anyway? I had found Tim Halpern, and from where I sat I could tell that I would need to start a whole new catagory for him—"top floor."

Tim's speech was over too soon. I had loved the sound of his voice, a voice that had been echoing in my memory for weeks, and I had loved staring at him. I cheered wildly with the rest of his contingent.

I was sitting next to Jane Hartley, whom I had met on my way into the auditorium. She clapped quietly.

"What do you think?" she asked me as we waited for our turn to file out of the assembly.

"Tim Halpern seems pretty good," I said, keeping my answer vague.

"He is kind of cute," she agreed. "Besides, Linda Mullen and Brian Jacoby are such nerds."

So we agreed after all, the two great political minds that we were. Tim Halpern was our boy. The trouble was, I wasn't sure that I wanted to share him.

Gram's spaghetti and meat sauce dinner that night was delicious, made even better by the fantasy that Tim was sitting with us in one of the empty chairs at the huge table. Just as we were finishing, Susan called on the phone.

"Want to come over on Sunday? We can play cards and just mess around," she invited. "My folks are going out."

"Sounds like fun."

"What are you doing tomorrow?" she asked.

"I was thinking about having my hair trimmed, but Christopher at Salon Elegant is so scissors happy, I'm always afraid I might be scalped."

"I go to Ann at Trimmings, and I love her." Susan did have a great haircut, but her hair was short and curly. Mine was long and wavy.

"Do you think she can do a good job with long hair?"

"Yes, I know she can. I've seen her do Laurel Mayer's hair."

"Is she the girl with the hair down to her waist?"

"Yes." Susan gave me the phone number. "Wish I could come, but I have to do some stuff with my mother," she complained.

"By the way, what did you think of the student government candidates?" I asked hesitantly.

"Oh, there's no question that Linda Mullen is the only reasonable choice."

"You're kidding."

"No. She's the only one interested in making the student government a responsible, decision-making organization. She wants to start a review board and a fair-discipline committee. Didn't you like her?"

"Well, her speech was kind of . . . er . . . hard to take."

"Yes," Susan agreed, "she could use help with her speech writing and delivery. I bet you could really give her a hand."

"Actually, I didn't think she was the best candidate," I responded, wondering how much to reveal.

"Who then? Brian Jacoby?"

"Actually, Tim Halpern seemed pretty good."

"Barbara, don't tell me you've fallen for a pretty face."

"I think I have," I admitted.

"Well, time will tell," she philosophized. "Let me know how you feel after you hear a few more of his speeches. Sports are his thing, and I suspect they are his only thing. Wind him up, and he throws the ball."

"Susan, that's awful," I complained. "Just because I haven't slung mud at your candidate, don't think there isn't any!"

"You're right. I'm sorry Barb. I'll see you Sunday. I've got to finish some of my homework so I can leave Sunday free."

"Good idea," I agreed. "See you then."

When we hung up, I polished off my geometry homework. I can't say the job I did was inspired. Inspiration came later in the evening when I slept in a collage of dreams. Every picture I saw had the same wonderful theme: Tim and I playing intramural volleyball, Tim and I at the movies, Tim and I at the senior prom.

4

The next morning after breakfast I dialed the number for Trimmings, hoping I could get an appointment with Ann.

"We have a ten o'clock cancellation, if you can make it," said the voice at the other end.

"I'll be there," I promised.

I rushed to get my bag and say goodbye to Gram. "I'm going down to have a haircut," I told her. "See you later."

"Okay, dear, do you need a ride?" With her chin cupped in her hands, her pencil poised as she gazed intently at a crossword puzzle, I could see she was going to have trouble tearing herself away.

"No, I can take my bike."

Trimmings, sparsely decorated in shades of beige, was a terrific change from Salon Elegant, and Ann turned out to be a tiny woman in her mid-twenties with short, dark, dramatically cut hair. The trim she gave me was so great that when I left, my hair actually looked longer and thicker than before I went in.

Elated, I browsed through some of the nearby clothing shops and ate lunch at the Hamburger Choo Choo before I unchained my bike from the sidewalk in front of Trimmings. Then a weird thing happened. Sandy Moore walked by as I was getting on my bike, and though I was feeling as though it might be fun to say hello, he just gave me a wave and kept on going. It was as if he didn't know me, and I couldn't figure out why. Oh well, maybe I'd see Tim on the way home. That's who I really wanted to see anyway, but no such luck. I rode slowly, and when I got back to the house, Gram was still sitting in that same chair in the den working on the crossword puzzle.

"Barbara, sweetheart. What time is it?" She looked up suddenly.

"Nearly one."

"Oh dear, you must be famished."

"I ate downtown at the Choo Choo."

"Hmm. Let me see your hair." I spun myself around so it would fan out like on a TV commercial.

"That's a haircut?" she wanted to know. "Who payed who?"

"Gram!" I was outraged. She squinted her eyes at me.

"Actually, it does look nice," she conceded.

Upstairs, I studied myself in the full-length mirror. With my new haircut I looked pretty good, I thought, but nevertheless, dressed in my overalls, running shoes, and sweatshirt, I could hardly be mistaken for a femme fatale. Maybe I should write to *Mademoiselle* magazine and see if they could turn me into a glamour girl. No, all I would have to do is spend a few hours with Mom. She would be delighted to show me everything I needed to know about using makeup.

Then I remembered the silver scoop-neck sweater with sparkles that she had brought back from her last trip. She had raved about how gorgeous I looked in it, but I had felt absolutely indecent, especially when I bent over. When she had finished admiring me, I took it off and hid it away in my bottom drawer.

Now, I pulled it out and held it up to me, smoothing out the wrinkles. Standing in front of the mirror, I wondered if I would dare wear it to school. Never, I decided, as I bundled it up and put it back in the drawer.

Okay, so I had cleaned up my act, but now it was too clean. I thought of a fuzzy blue sweater and chocolate velour slacks I had seen that morning. Tim would certainly notice me in that outfit. Maybe I should ride back downtown and try them on. I could charge them to Mom. I knew she'd be pleased.

So much for homework that day. I got back on my bike and rode to The Heather Tree. But I didn't buy the fuzzy blue, after all. It fit okay, but I just couldn't picture myself walking around school in it.

I ended up buying a beautiful lavender plaid blouse with a lace collar and lavender socks. Then I went next door to the army-navy store and bought a pair of taupe-colored corduroy jeans to match. The velour ones had been cut all wrong for me.

Putting the two packages in the side baskets of my bike, I realized what I had done. I had set out to make some daring, eye-catching purchases, and ended up with another comfortable plaid shirt and pair of jeans, not all that different from what I had always worn. I had failed in the first step of my self-imposed transformation.

The next morning when I got up, there was a note in the kitchen from Gram to say she had gone to the library. Since Jonathan had stayed overnight at his friend Mike's, I ate my breakfast in blissful silence. Later, when I went next door to Susan's, she noticed my haircut right away.

"Your hair looks nice," she told me. "How do you like it?"

"Fine, but now I'm wondering if I should have let her do something more dramatic."

"Such as?"

"I don't know. Ann herself has a terrific haircut. It's hard to explain. Lately, I've been thinking it would be nice to try a big change. But listen to what happened yesterday." I told her how I had gone shopping specifically to buy spiffy clothes and ended up with more of what I already had. "And this is the shirt."

"I like it," Susan told me, "but it's hardly Ann's style."

"I know. I just keep feeling I'm in a rut."

"Don't be silly. You wear what feels like you. Ann wears what's her."

"I guess you're right," I confessed, "but maybe it's time to grow up."

"But even grown-up," Susan persisted, "you'll still be Barbara Lane. I don't think you'd ever be happy being someone other than yourself. Besides, I'd hate it if you were Ann the haircutter."

"Or Laurel Mayer?" I tried out.

"Yuck. Why would you want to be her?"

"I don't know," I lied. "Long blond hair seems awful nice."

"Barbara, make up your mind! Do you want short dramatic hair, or do you want it straight and long?"

"Oh, Susan, I don't really know!"

Monday morning I dressed carefully for school in my new corduroy jeans and a black turtleneck sweater. It was a color my mother wore a lot, and I felt very sophisticated. Susan had gone in early for driver's ed class, so I walked to school alone, enjoying the cool October air.

The halls in school were plastered with campaign posters: "Linda Mullen, the sane alternative"; "Brian Jacoby for President"; and finally, "Tim, Tim, he's our guy. He's just what we need at North Hollow High." I was almost late for homeroom because I was so distracted by all the signs.

But in addition to studying the posters, my eyes darted back and forth through the crowds of kids in hopes of finding Tim as I climbed the stairs.

I was almost late for study hall too, so intense was my search, and the bell was ringing as I slipped into my seat as unobtrusively as I could. Sandy was already there, his long legs crossed, twirling his ankle in time to some unheard music. He was deep at work in his black-covered sketchbook, which suddenly reminded me of my own maroon journal.

He was wearing his usual battered jeans, a stretched-out sweat shirt, and running shoes without socks. And it was freezing out! How could he?

He didn't even bother to give me his familiar brief nod, so I pulled some paper from my notebook and took out a pen, determined to write a letter to Jennifer. But the silver-painted study hall radiators were making loud clanking sounds, filling the air with dusty stifling steam. Suddenly, I wished I had left my socks home, too. Mrs. Bradshaw had been thoughtful enough to leave the door open, and fascinated, I watched people straggle by the door.

I looked down at my paper, but I wasn't sure how to start my letter, so I ended up staring out the door again, wondering where Tim might be.

Then, there he was. In an instant, Tim floated by as if he had read my mind. I didn't get a clear view, of course. It's not as if he stopped and waved, but I did see a strong figure with dark hair, dressed in a muted striped shirt, that was unmistakably Tim.

That was all I needed to send me off into a delicious reverie. There we were, Tim and I, walking down the hall, hand in hand. Tim was going to basketball practice, and he kissed me goodbye as I went off to the newspaper office to write my latest story.

It was another of my fabulous fantasies, and when I felt a gentle tapping on my foot, I focused back on reality to find Sandy had deposited a scrap of notebook paper on my desk. Automatically, my eyes flickered up to Bradshaw, but her attention was elsewhere. We were safe.

Moving the scrap of paper around so I could see the printing, I read "Shall we abolish classes for sports? I'll nominate you for captain of the volleyball team." Wondering what he meant, I shifted his note to discover I had written, "Tim, Tim, he's our guy," all over the paper I had meant for Jennifer's letter.

"He's got to be the best candidate," I defended on the same scrap of paper, which I deftly slipped back onto Sandy's desk. We both knew who I meant.

"It all depends on what you want from student government. I never figured you for the rah-rah set," Sandy returned on the same scrap. Bradshaw was immersed in a big fat book, I was relieved to see, but I was still sweating.

"That's not at all the issue. He plans to raise money for the entire school to use, not just the sports teams."

"We'll have to wait and see about that."

"Who are you voting for?"

"Mullen."

"She hasn't got a prayer against Tim."

"It pains me to admit it, but you're probably right about that."

"We'll see next week," I gloated. So at least Sandy admitted that I had picked a winner. It made me feel good, and I thought I had made a good, quick defense and cover-up.

Sandy had suddenly opened his French text and seemed to be studying, so I got to work on my letter to Jennifer. Note writing with Sandy had gotten me in the mood. I only wished Jennifer's answer, if it ever arrived, would be as much fun to read as Sandy's.

The rest of the day passed quickly. I ate lunch with Jane Hartley in the cafeteria. A little on the dull side, she's nice enough. I wasn't really up for calculator talk with Susan's crowd, and I didn't want to risk being cornered by Susan's friend Joy, who had been suffocatingly attentive since she realized that Barbara Lane was, in fact, the daughter of Claire West and Martin Lane.

In English, Rush had the good taste to be out sick, and the substitute just gave us an essay test. Not a bad way to spend forty minutes, I thought, although a lot of kids groaned out loud when the assignment was announced. I rushed through, and then sat at my desk wondering about Tim. Where was he? What was his class schedule? Where was his locker? Would I see him again that day? Would I have the nerve to say something to him?

I did see Tim again that day, in the hall just before I left for home. That's the good news. He was surrounded by a group of cheerleader types, Laurel Mayer being one of them. That's the bad news.

So, there was no way I could contrive to introduce myself to him Monday. Any plans I had worked up about pretending to bump into him went right out the window. I wasn't prepared to make a fool of myself in front of all those girls, but that afternoon glimpse I got was enough to send me home several inches above the ground. Seeing Tim twice in one day was almost more than my senses could stand.

I was so wrapped up in dreams of Tim that I had forgotten my folks were due home that evening. We were reading *Diary of Anne Frank* for history, which Mrs. Harris had assured us was much more meaningful than memorizing dates from our text. After wondering whether I'd be able to put Tim out of my mind long enough to read a few chapters, I got so wrapped up in the story, I lost all sense of time. Immersed in Anne's frightening reality, I was both frustrated and relieved to be interrupted several hours later by my mother's musical voice ringing up the stairs.

"Darlings, we're home." Turning over my book, I ran downstairs to greet them.

Gram and Jonathan were already there hugging Mom and Dad. Michael was carrying in their bags.

"Look at Barbara," crooned Mom, giving me a sweet-smelling hug and kiss. "You look wonderful honey; so grown-up." Mom looked so elegant in her red dress, it was hard to believe she had just stepped off an airplane.

I turned to be hugged and kissed by my father. Nearly as splashy-looking as Mom, he wore a navy sport jacket with brass buttons, white shirt, and a printed silk ascot around his neck. "We missed you kids so much," he told us. "It's great to be home. Barbara, regards to you from your friend Seth," he told me, passing along what he probably thought was an innocent comment.

Inside, I shuddered. Since the night of Mom and Dad's big New York concert, I had erased Seth Guild from my mind.

We all sat down together in the big dining room for the first time in nearly two months. Gram served a steak dinner.

"I met an old college buddy on the plane this trip who has a top-notch recording studio in New York," Dad announced suddenly. "He's a great guy, really, and I'm going to look into transferring some of our work into his place. If everything works out, we'll be home a lot more from now on. Such an amazing coincidence. T.J.'s been living here in North Hollow for years, and it takes a trip to L.A. to find him."

That's because you're hardly ever around, I

thought to myself, but Gram was surprisingly diplomatic. "Sounds like good news if ever I've heard it," she said. "What's the fellow's name, Martin?"

"T.J., T.J. Halpern. We played basketball together at school." Dad was off reminiscing about his college days, and I went numb.

"Barb, honey, are you okay? You're not eating?"

"I'm fine, Mom, really. Just thinking."

"How's school, dear?"

"Oh fine. Better."

"Are you ready for me to pursue Lloyd's? I'll call them first thing tomorrow morning, if you like."

"Uh, that's okay, Mom. Thanks. Actually, things are much much better. I don't think I want to bother with Lloyd's now."

"Barbara, are you all right?" She really sounded concerned, but I didn't want to miss any of what Dad was saying.

"So anyway, T.J. looks exactly the same," Dad was finishing up, "except for the spare tire around his middle." He patted his own flat stomach.

"Does he have a family?" Gram wanted to know. Leave it to her to get to the heart of the matter.

"Yes, a lovely wife, Gloria, who also went to school with us, and a son who, I think, goes to North Hollow High. Barb, do you know anyone named Halpern?"

"There's a Tim Halpern running for school president, and he's a basketball player, too, I think, but I don't know him personally." It was hard to seem nonchalant.

"Must be one and the same," Dad concluded, "named for his father, Timothy James."

"Jonathan, dear, how's school?" Mom cut in,

mercifully changing the subject and giving me time to digest this startling new information.

Later that evening, as I was getting ready for bed, Mom came in with a silver-wrapped box for me. I started to open it, hoping to find something to wear inside that was smashing, but not too smashing, if you know what I mean. Mom tackled me again.

"Barbara, tell me more about school. Why this sudden turnabout."

"Well, Mom, I thought I wouldn't be able to stand some of my teachers, but it's turning out better than I thought." There was no way I was going to mention that finding Tim was really what made me change my mind about leaving North Hollow.

"Is it just better, or is it really good?"

"I'm not sure. Better to almost good."

"Is there anything I can do to help improve it? Can I speak to the principal or something?"

"No. Actually, Mom, I'd really prefer if you'd stay out of it," I blurted. "It's hard enough when people find out who my parents are."

"Whatever do you mean?"

I took a deep breath. "I'm not sure if you can understand this, and I do love you, but sometimes people have funny ideas about you when you have famous parents."

"And so you would rather I didn't throw my weight around?"

"Exactly."

"Okay. I read you, but I do wish I could do something for you, Barbie. You just haven't seemed happy since you started at the high school. And your grades, not that they ever meant much to me, used to be so good. Do you miss Jennifer a lot?"

"Pretty much," I told her, "but I'm getting used to it, and I have a new friend, Susan. Her folks bought the Mitchell's house, and she's really terrific."

"That's good news, anyway. Meantime, I'm going to be around much more now, and I really am here to do what I can for you."

"Thanks, Mom."

"And Barbara, don't forget the package," she reminded me. I looked down to see the half-opened pretty silver box, which was still in my lap. Tearing off the rest of the paper, I found a terrific magenta sweat shirt inside, printed with little pink-and-green flowers.

"It's great Mom, I love it," I told her, and it was, in fact, just the kind of thing I had been hoping for. "Thanks a lot. Do you mind if I wait until tomorrow to try it on?" I apologized, "I'm really pooped."

"Fine, fine, and goodnight, honey." She gave me a big kiss and left.

What I couldn't tell her was that I needed time alone to sort things out. My father and Tim's were old college pals. What did this mean to me? Should I run up to him in school tomorrow, throw my arms around him, and yell, "Tim, this is fate. This was meant to be." No, that really was too tasteless. But nevertheless, our fathers were old friends. Could I somehow use that to my advantage? No, I couldn't do it, not even in my wildest fantasies. I knew I had to keep the boy of my dreams separate from what a lot of people considered dream parents.

It was hard, at first, having Mom and Dad home. Mornings weren't all that different because they were still asleep when I left for school, but the rest of the time they expected me to be like them, chatty and cheerful. All I wanted to do was lock myself in my room and think about Tim.

It devastates me to admit that nothing changed at all that first week after my parents got back. I saw Tim in the hall at school a lot, but he was always surrounded by mobs of people, and I never got to say one word to him. He did win the election, though, which was no surprise, and in study hall Sandy Moore commemorated the event with a nasty cartoon of the school being bulldozed down to make way for a new, high-tech gymnasium.

Cheerleading tryouts had been announced that week, too. I gave some thought to trying out and practiced one afternoon in what I thought was the privacy of my own room. Barging in just as I was waving my fists over my head, Jonathan asked delicately, "Cheerleading for chimpanzees?"

"Get out of my room!" I shrieked.

But I knew he was right. Grace was not one of my chief assets. So much for that fantasy.

5

I've invited T.J. and his family to dinner next Friday night," Dad announced over dessert. "Is that a problem for anyone? Claire? Lenore? Barbara and Jonathan, I'd like you to be here, too." He looked around the table at all of us, waiting for nods of agreement. I felt as though he had just dropped a bomb on my head.

"Fine, dear," Mom assured him.

"Lenore?" He turned to my grandmother, "I'd be delighted if you would have someone cater. I certainly don't intend this to be a headache for you."

"Oh Martin, don't be silly," Gram protested. "You know how I love to cook for these festive occasions."

Dad turned to us. "Barb, Jon, anything important for next Friday night?"

"I have cub scouts," Jonathan volunteered.

"That's over at four thirty, stupid!" I reminded him.

"Barbara, and you?"

"Nothing Dad. It sounds fine." Inside I was flashing hot and cold. It was better than fine. It was fantastic—but how could I tell him that?

Afterward, I left the dinner table and went to my room in a reverie. Friday night was a whole week away. I'd have all that time to plan just what I'd say to Tim once I had him on my home territory. Would he like me? How could I make myself as exciting as Laurel Mayer? Maybe I could get my hair to grow three feet overnight and dye it blonde. And what would I wear? My mind raced back and forth, and I found answers to none of my questions.

The next day, Saturday, I went to see Susan, who was sitting in her room. "You're weird today," she told me.

"What do you mean?"

"You're only half here. Where's the rest of you?" she wanted to know.

"Well, uh—" How could I deny it? How could I say Tim is coming to my house for dinner and I have to think about it every moment? Susan would probably laugh at me.

"Barbara, is it that hard having your parents at home?"

"Well, uh—" Now I was feeling really dumb.

"I know it's a touchy subject," she went on, "but since your parents got back, you've been floating further and further away—just the way you were a couple of months back, but not as bad, of course. At least you're still taking care of the way you look."

"It is a little hard to have them around," I admitted. "Having two overpowering personalities in the house can really be a turnoff."

"Barbara, they're your parents!"

"I know, I know. It's so hard to explain. But listen to Dad's latest. He bumped into an old college friend the other day, someone he hadn't seen in twenty years, and invited him and his family to dinner. He insists that we be there, too. Isn't that heavy."

"It could be," she admitted, "but you'll probably never see them again afterward, so don't worry about it."

"Oh, you're probably right," I agreed, trying to keep my tone light as I realized the truth of what she said. After one night together, I might never see Tim again. "But you'll never guess in a million years whose family it is."

"Well, give me a hint, at least. Is it someone I know?"

"Sort of, a boy we both know from school. A big shot."

"Barbara, I really have no idea."

"Okay, okay. It's the Halpern Family."

"As in Tim Halpern, super jock and school president?" She was incredulous.

"Yes," I laughed. "Do you believe it? Dad used to play basketball with Mr. Halpern."

"So you get to meet our illustrious leader first-hand. Aren't you thrilled?" Her tone was sarcastic. This, I knew, was definitely not the time to tell Susan what was on my mind. "Maybe you could get your grandmother to cook something absolutely poisonous and put Tim out of commission for a while," she continued. "A lot of kids at North Hollow would thank you."

"Susan, that's revolting."

"I know," she confessed, "but Linda Mullen is in my history class, and she's senior class representative. She says Tim is turning out to be really irresponsible, and the rest of the kids are getting really disgusted."

"How can that be?" I defended. "He's only been president a week; Linda's just jealous."

"Maybe so," Susan allowed.

Though I waited patiently all weekend for school to resume, I didn't see Tim on Monday or Tuesday, much to my disappointment. He was busy working on student government, I hoped. But a few times, I did see Laurel Mayer off in a corner of the lawn helping a friend with her cheers. Laurel, with her extravagant blond hair, had made the team last year. Her pretty friend with dark shoulder-length hair, sort of like mine, was wearing bright red lipstick and gobs of eye makeup, very much in Laurel's style. I watched them as long as I dared. The unknown girl looked good, I thought, and I wondered who she was.

Everywhere I turned in school, I saw groups of girls practicing for cheerleading tryouts. Even though I had come to accept as unrealistic my fantasy of making the team, I was still perversely interested in who was trying out.

Tuesday morning, as I sat in study hall trying to concentrate on my French, it was impossible to get anything done. Radiators clanking, the heat was up full blast, and Mrs. Bradshaw had mercifully left the front door of the study hall open. From down the hall came an echo of "Rah Ed, Rah Payne, Rah, Rah, Ed Payne." It was the cheer that would have to be perfected for tryouts.

Bradshaw rushed out of the room to apprehend the noise makers. Turning to Sandy to see if he had enjoyed her blustering exit, I saw he was busy at work on a drawing, which I hoped he would show me. I was just in the mood for his sarcastic humor.

While Sandy was still working, Bradshaw steamed back into the room with a satisfied smile on her face and sat down at her desk. In the last few weeks, we had perfected our note-passing techniques, and I'm proud to say we had not been caught by the ever-vigilant Bradshaw.

But this time, I lost control. When Sandy's cartoon arrived, I saw that he had drawn a row of cheerleaders kicking their legs up in the air, chorus-line style. Dressed in North Hollow's traditional short skirt, sweater, socks, and saddle shoes, they all had ridiculous animal faces—a donkey, a pig, a cow, a dog, a goat, and a few other creatures. One cheerleader, I noticed, had just an outline for a head. Sandy had left it blank, and underneath was a note that said, "Wouldn't you like to join the team?"

I was shocked. How could Sandy know what had been on my mind? It was impossible. Realizing he must have been joking, I wrote underneath his note, "Certainly, but what animal could I be?"

Sandy made a few quick lines and slipped the note back onto my desk. That's when I blew it. Looking down at the drawing, I searched through the animal faces to see how I had been portrayed. When I saw what he had done, I sat back, closed my eyes, and let out a giggle that echoed back and forth across the study hall.

Sandy had made me a striped cat, an image that pleased me until I thought of Gram's fat beast Cindy dressed in a short red-and-black cheerleader's jumper and saddle shoes.

I opened my eyes to hear Bradshaw demand, "What's so funny?" Silence followed, and I knew she was scanning her seating chart for my name. "Lane, bring whatever you're reading up here," she commanded.

I turned Sandy's note facedown and stuck it between the pages of my French text as the two of us walked up the aisle. But she pulled out the piece of paper soon enough and turned it over to examine Sandy's drawing.

"You two do realize that study hall is for schoolwork, not note passing."

"Yes, Mrs. Bradshaw," we both answered.

"Fine," she told us, "then it will come as no surprise when I invite you both to detention this Friday afternoon." We were silent. "Well?" she demanded harshly.

"Yes, Mrs. Bradshaw," we answered in unison.

"Good, and I need not remind you of the consequences should you fail to appear promptly at three o'clock."

"No, Mrs. Bradshaw," we responded.

"Go back to your seats, then, and get to work."

We stepped sheepishly off her platform and trailed down the aisle, but Bradshaw is such a creature of ridicule, it's hard to feel humiliated for very long. As for detention itself, what was another hour of silent contemplation!

Sandy thought the whole experience funny, so much so that he got to work on another drawing as soon as we got back to our desks. Slipping the sketch onto my desk in just a few minutes, I saw he had drawn Bradshaw the Bat flying around the study hall with ghoulish glowing eyes and a million little disgusting teeth. Like a fool, I let out another amused chuckle. I must have been mad. How could I suddenly lose my self-control?

"Lane and Moore," commanded Bradshaw across the room, "Friday detention, *two* hours. Now, no more from either of you, or you'll be there all weekend."

Sandy and I smirked at each other, and I finally opened my French book, Friday afternoon, two hours, echoing in my head. If I get into any more hot water with Bradshaw, I might miss dinner with Tim altogether! The thought was so horrible that suddenly I was able to concentrate on my French vocabulary words.

When the bell finally rang, releasing us from Bradshaw's clutches, Sandy, in his usual way, vanished before I could say a word to him. Walking down to geometry class, I thought of that day a few weeks back when I had passed him on the downtown sidewalk. He had barely said hello, but that was weeks ago. Now, after weeks of sharing notes, I knew something was definitely wrong. Was Sandy Moore afraid of me because of my parents? It was so probable, it made me sick.

Mom wanted to go clothes-shopping with me Tuesday after school, but I just wasn't in the mood.

"Are you tired, sweetie?" she wanted to know.

"No, just too much homework, and I had kind of

a bad day." I ran up the stairs before she could question me any more. I certainly didn't want to get caught with her in the middle of an idol-worship scene in a department store. I said little at dinner that night, despite Mom's efforts to draw me out of my gloom.

"Don't mind me," I warned Susan the next morning on the way to school. "I feel really rotten."

"What's the matter?"

"Oh, everything." I told her about my odd correspondence friendship with Sandy. "I think maybe he's afraid of me because of Mom and Dad," I confessed. "I know you think I imagine these things, but when people find out about them, sometimes they start acting weird. Have you ever noticed how Joy started coming on to me when she realized?"

"Yes, and I'm sorry for it," she apologized as if she were guilty of something.

"Don't be silly. It's not your fault. I just mentioned it so you'd realize I wasn't making things up. And I am sad about Sandy. He seems like such a fun guy, but he just won't talk to me."

"Lots of fun," she laughed. "He gets the two of you sentenced to two hours of detention."

"That's nothing," I defended. "You know Bradshaw is a real lunatic."

"Well, then, maybe he's just plain shy," she suggested. "Just go easy, and enjoy things the way they are. Anyway, I'm glad to see you're interested in somebody other than that super-creep Tim Halpern."

"Are you kidding?" I started and then shut my mouth. How could I let her know the truth? Sandy just seemed like a nice guy, somebody fun to joke around with. Tim would always be the boy of my dreams.

Sandy was absent from study hall that morning, and I suspected he had taken a library pass. Was he avoiding me? I opened my French book to cram for the big test, consoling myself with the thought that at least he wasn't there to distract me.

I barely made it through the week.

"Miss Lane, this paper is an abomination," announced Mr. Rush in a loud voice as he handed me back my test essay in English class that Friday afternoon.

With Tim on my mind, I hadn't been paying much attention to my schoolwork. So the "F" at the top of my paper came as no surprise. I held my breath, waiting to see if his familiar humiliating tirade would follow, but none came. Rush continued to move around the room, handing back papers to their owners with comments of praise and damnation.

What a relief. Friday, of all days, I was in no mood for his games. I wanted nothing to interfere with my excitement about dinner. There was one little problem of course. At three o'clock I had to sit for two glorious hours in detention.

"Third row, Lane," commanded Bradshaw, when I walked in later in the afternoon, indicating a seat in an isolated corner. Sandy arrived moments later; she assigned him to a desk across the room from me. Watching him take his place, I saw him look quickly around the room. Was he looking for me? I wondered, relieved that he was too far away to tempt me into trouble.

The minutes of silence ticked by, and I opened

Moby Dick, resigned to making inroads with that masterpiece of boredom. I made great progress, but after an hour and a half, I had to stop. I glanced across to Sandy, who suddenly looked up and gave me a big wink before diving back into his own reading. I was completely puzzled.

I continued to watch him, fairly confident that once he had been bold enough to give me such an uncharacteristic wink, it would take him some time to build up the nerve to look back. And I was right. As I sat staring, his face, obscured by long stringy hair, never again left the pages of his book.

When the clock finally hit five P.M., Bradshaw announced the end of detention, and I got up slowly, stiff from sitting so long. Stretching my muscles, I was surprised to find Sandy at my side as I left study hall and headed for my locker.

"Now wasn't that a gas?" he asked. "Wouldn't you like to do that more often?"

"Not really," I told him, annoyed that he was interfering with my efforts to get home quickly. The Halperns were arriving at seven o'clock, and I needed every spare minute to get ready.

"I've signed you up for next Friday's detention too," Sandy continued to joke, but his attempt to be funny only made me more irritable.

"Great," I said, "Now you'll have to excuse me. I have to get home for dinner."

"It's only five o'clock," he challenged. "Don't tell me you eat this early."

"No, actually dinner's at seven," I admitted, "but I have to get dressed."

"Two hours to get dressed? My, my, my."

"We're having company," I finally confessed.

"Must be awfully important if you need all that time to wash your face. The President and the First Lady perhaps?"

"Don't be stupid!"

"S-O-R-R-Y," he defended.

I knew I had hurt his feelings, because he was backing away. "It's rather funny," I told him in an attempt to make amends. "It's an old friend that my father hasn't seen since college who is coming with his family, and his name is T.J. Halpern."

"That sounds familiar," mused Sandy. "Any relation to our illustrious president?"

"Yes, that's the funny part. It's Tim Halpern's father."

"Tim Halpern is coming to your house for dinner?" Sandy was incredulous.

"Yes, isn't that a riot?" Without thinking, I had revealed to Sandy my deepest, darkest secret.

"So, that's why you have to rush home to get ready," speculated Sandy.

"Yes," I concluded firmly, slamming my locker door and heading down the hall by myself. "See ya."

When I got home and opened the front door, I was overwhelmed by cooking smells, and I rushed into the kitchen to see what was happening. Gram was bent over the oven basting something enormous, and Serena, our part-time housekeeper, was unwrapping the good silverware.

"Smells good," I told Gram. "What is it?"

"A turkey, dear, with all the trimmings."

"Mmm," I said, hoping to sound enthusiastic.

Worrying that Gram's turkey might fulfill Susan's request after all, I went upstairs. Mom was in her room humming softly, so I stuck my head in to say hello. She was sitting at her dressing table in a bright blue kimono putting on makeup.

"Hi sweetie," she greeted, catching sight of me in her mirror. "All set for dinner?"

"I will be," I promised. "But Mom, about Gram? Did you know she's making another turkey? What if it's inedible again?"

"Barbara, don't worry. Serena's down there helping. Now run along and get ready. Would you like a little help with your hair or makeup or anything?"

"Thanks Mom, I would. I'll take a quick shower, and then I'll be back."

"Fine, dear."

I had spent days thinking about what I would wear for this major event in my life, but once showered and hair blown dry, I stood in front of my closet in my underwear trying to make a last minute decision.

Finally settling on my denim skirt and plum-colored sweater with a slightly low neck, I went back to Mom's room to ask her for help with my hair. Now dressed in scarlet slacks and a flowing white silk blouse, on one arm were about a hundred gold bracelets, and at her ears were big gold baubles.

"Barbara, why so gloomy?" she asked, examining what I wore. "I thought you had decided on that outfit that we just bought?"

"It just didn't feel right when I put it on. I think I need to have it taken in."

"But we had plenty of time for that."

"I know, but it didn't seem that way when we bought it," I confessed.

"Oh well, let's see what we can do with your hair," she said, looking at me with squinty eyes. Directing me to her dressing table, she tried several things with my hair, finally brushing it over the top of my head on one side and pinning it with a small clip. I never would have thought to do it myself, and I had to admit it looked pretty good.

Surveying her work, she seemed pleased, too. "How about a little mascara and blusher?" she asked, "just for a little extra drama."

"Fine, Mom. But not too much."

"Don't be silly. At fifteen, you hardly need any. You have your own natural beauty." Just like a mother, I thought, as I closed my eyes and felt her dab at my eyelashes.

The Halperns arrived like a giant wave a few minutes after seven P.M., and their presence flooded the house. Introducing me, Dad said, "T.J. and Gloria, this is my daughter Barbara." Mr. Halpern was dressed in a dark business suit much like Dad's, except his pot belly made him look about ten years older, and Mrs. Halpern wore a fancy but dowdy navy dress with matching shoes.

"We're glad to meet you," said Mr. Halpern in a voice that boomed almost as loud as Dad's. Mrs. Halpern, who was actually a rather pretty blond woman, gave me a wan smile that I suspected was her best effort. "And here," continued Mr. Halpern, taking my hand and pulling me forward, "is my best son, Timmy." As far as I knew, Tim was their only son so I laughed at what must have been a joke as I looked up at Tim. I had never been so close to him before, and I nearly lost my breath. The blue-gray crewneck sweater he wore was a perfect complement to his transparent skin and green eyes, subtleties that were impossible to detect from far away.

"Hi," I said dumbly.

"Glad to meet you," answered Tim, before turning away to be introduced to Jonathan.

Mom herded us all into the living room, where she could take drink orders and offer the Halperns some caviar pie, one of the few things she made herself. "Barbara, sweets, run into the kitchen for some orange juice, will you, and ask Gram to come relax with us." I was only too happy to have a chance to leave. I needed a few minutes to get my head together.

Dad and Mr. Halpern spent the first part of the evening talking about old times at their college fraternity house and reliving favorite old basketball games they had played together. Tim, seemingly interested in learning every detail of their athletic conquests, egged them on with questions like, "and what did the referee say," and "how many stitches did you need?"

But as much as I wanted to hear everything Tim said, basketball became so boring that I found myself tuning in to Mom's efforts to draw out Mrs. Halpern.

"So, Gloria, Marty tells me you were at school with the boys, too, or is that a well-guarded secret? You certainly look too young to have been in their class."

"Well, I was only a freshman when they were seniors," Mrs. Halpern explained with a straight face, Mom's attempt to be lighthearted going right past her.

"And what are you doing with yourself these days?" Mom pursued.

"Well, I'm redoing the living room this season," said Mrs. Halpern, "and in my leisure time I'm very active with the garden club." Now, here was a subject Mom could get into, and I let their conversation fade as soon as I started hearing words like "rototill" and "mulch."

So there I sat, stuck between basketball and gardening. The evening was slipping away and with it was going my golden opportunity to get to know Tim.

6

During dinner I consoled myself that once we moved into the den, a more intimate room, I would have my chance to approach Tim, who so far had said nothing to me beyond hello. After all, how much longer could this preoccupation with basketball go on?

But once in the den, Tim and Mom became engrossed in a conversation of their own; Mr. and Mrs. Halpern went off to a corner to chat with Dad; Jonathan disappeared to the kitchen on some unknown mission; and Gram was directing Serena in the dining room.

"Mrs. Lane, I can't tell you what a thrill this is to meet you," Tim was telling Mom; "we have all your albums, and I just heard your new single on the radio—"Dreams," I think it's called—and it's by far the best thing you and Mr. West have ever done."

"Thank you, dear," Mom was saying, "It's Marty's composition, you know."

Tim had a million questions about her career, which Mom seemed delighted to answer. I sat down and stared, impressed by Tim's ease.

Still, I felt like an invisible visitor from Mars. It was as if I wasn't there. Mr. Halpern and Mrs. Halpern had each given me a smile or two, but from Tim I had gotten absolutely no reaction. Frustration was turning to pure pain when Mr. Halpern finally ignited the spark I had so badly wanted.

"Yes, our Timmy is an important fellow at the high school," he announced to Dad, "Recently elected president of the student government, you know, as well as being captain of a champion basketball team."

"Barbara, you never told us," chastised Dad.

"Sure I did, Dad, and I even voted for you, Tim," I announced, bravely looking Tim in the eyes.

"Thank you, Barbara," he answered modestly.

"Timmy, however do you have time for politics as well as sports?" questioned Mom.

"Oh, I find the time, Mrs. Lane," he answered. "There's a lot to get done, but the secret is in delegating responsibility," he continued. "With good people at the head of each group, there should be no problem."

"Ah, the classic problem," mused Dad, "finding good people."

"Yes," agreed Tim, "And I'm starting a full-scale fund-raising drive, a booster club, to raise money for travel expenses for our teams, new equipment, and, if there's anything extra, books for the library."

"Aren't you impressed, Marty!" demanded Mr. Halpern.

"Oh, very." Dad assured. "So Barbara, have you

volunteered to give Tim a hand with his worthwhile endeavors?"

"Wouldn't that almost be like old times, Marty," gushed Mr. Halpern, "to have our two kids working together like we did. Remember the winter carnival dance we ran way back when the band showed up two hours late?"

"Yes, and we ended up doing a few numbers ourselves. I sang, and you and John accompanied me with combs and waxed paper! What an earful we were." Dad's face was lit with pleasure.

"Even then you were a star!" laughed Mr. Halpern.

"Barbara, why don't you sign up for Tim's booster club?" urged Dad. "It would give you a little something to do, too, instead of moping around here all day." The nerve of my father! How would I ever survive this embarrassment?

"Dad, I'm really very busy with schoolwork," I said in my own defense.

"We really could use your help," confirmed Tim. "The biggest thing I'm planning to fill our bank account is a giant orange and grapefruit sale."

"What a novel idea," cooed Mom, "and such a nice change from magazines."

"Thanks," answered Tim, "I actually got the idea from a friend at Hilldown High. They raised several thousand dollars last year. Of course it's bound to be a major undertaking, so we need all the help we can get." Tim was looking at me with his bright green eyes.

"I'd be glad to give you a hand," I promised him easily.

"It would be great if we could count on you," he

said. "Now, the sales drive won't be beginning until after Christmas vacation; that's a while off, so listen for some announcement in school around then."

"Isn't that the beginning of basketball season, son?" asked Mr. Halpern.

"Yes, Dad, that's why it's important to recruit good people now." Tim gave me a smile bright enough to light a Christmas tree, and I filled with a warm glow.

"What a lovely evening," commented Mom after the Halperns left. "T.J. and his boy are just delightful."

"So glad you liked them, dear," said Dad.

"Lenore, the dinner was just delicious," Dad called out to Gram, who was putting away crystal in the hutch in the dining room. "I just wish you wouldn't work so hard."

"Serena and I have it all taken care of. This is the last of it."

Later that night, before I went to sleep, I went over every conversation he had during the evening with every person in my family, including the compliments he paid Gram on her chocolate mousse, which had come from the bakery downtown.

Admittedly, my own interchanges with him had been brief and reasonably unfulfilling. But these things didn't happen overnight. It would take time, and I was prepared to be patient.

After that fateful dinner party, Tim began waving to me in school whenever he noticed me nearby. "You know Tim?" questioned Jane one day, as she walked by my side, her eyes huge with envy.

"A little," I had to confess. "Our parents are

friends, and he came to dinner with them last week."

"So what's he like," Jane asked. "Is he as super as he seems?"

"Absolutely," I assured her, but beyond the thrill of receiving a friendly wave and smile, there was nothing more intimate.

Thanksgiving came and went, but nothing more changed between me and Tim. By the time Christmas arrived, Tim was still foremost in my mind, if not in my life, and I deserved a blue ribbon for my patience.

Although Mom and Dad had made plans to start recording at T.J. Halpern's New York studio, they still had to do a Christmas tour, for which they apologized profusely. As consolation, they offered to send us down to Florida to visit Gram's sister Hetty, who lived in a condominium on the beach. We had been there once before, and while Gram and Jonathan had a great time—Gram was glad to be with her sister, and Jonathan made friends with other visiting grandchildren—I had felt oppressed by the high-rise concrete vista that hung behind the crowded beach.

"Thanks for the offer, Dad, but I'd rather not go," I said, when he asked my opinion.

"You louse," hissed Jonathan. "Now I won't get to see all my neat friends or go to Disney World."

"I don't care if you go without me," I suggested. "My intention is not to spoil anyone's fun, JONATHAN." If looks could kill, he would have been a goner.

"Sweetie, you can't stay in the house alone," said

Mom, concerned. "Why not go visit Jennifer in Washington?"

As it turned out, I stayed at Susan's while the rest of my family was away. Twice a day, I went home to feed the cats.

Christmas came and went. I exchanged gifts with Susan and her family and opened the packages my mother had left behind for me. During the first few days of vacation, Susan and I went to the movies a few times, went shopping once, and took the train to New York City for a musical we both wanted to see. The weather was unseasonably warm, and although I knew Gram and Jonathan were on the beach in Florida, I was glad I had stayed in North Hollow, where there was always an inkling of a chance I might bump into Tim.

One morning, Susan left early for New York City to see a computer demonstration with Matthew, a cute guy she had met in school. Even though she had invited me over and over again to join them, and I knew she really meant it, there was no way I could bring myself to tag along.

"Thanks, but I've got to feed the cats at home, and then I'll probably call Jane and see if she wants to go to see *The Lady Vanishes* at the Art movie house," I told her.

"Haven't you ever seen that?" she asked surprised.

"Yes, about a million times on TV" I conceded, "but I'm sure it's really fantastic on a big movie screen without all those dumb commercials."

So I went next door to give the cats breakfast and call Jane. The cats, gobbling their food down in the kitchen, quickly appeared in my room for some serious petting, which I gave them as I dialed Jane's number. Her line was busy for about twenty minutes though, and while I was waiting to try again, I noticed that I had left my journal, usually stored away in my vanity, sitting on the table next to the telephone.

I hadn't written anything in it for at least a week, so when the cats finally fell asleep contentedly on my bed, I picked it up, ready to start a new entry. Mostly, I had been writing a lot of free-form stuff about Tim, but since I hadn't seen him all vacation, there was nothing new to say. Maybe I would try something a little different, something that would be more of a challenge.

I began jotting down ideas about an imaginary girl, new at North Hollow High and afraid of her own shadow. It was fun to invent a character whom I knew something about, but who really wasn't me. As I wrote, a story started to come into my mind, and I got completely absorbed in what I was doing.

It would be a short story, I decided, and Tim would be the friendly boy at school who helps my heroine overcome her shyness.

Once I made the decision to write an official short story, I began to work on looseleaf paper. First I wrote a plot outline, and then I made notes on the characters I would include in the action.

Sheets and sheets of paper ended up in the garbage as I experimented with sentences, and as paragraphs finally began to form, I began to get excited. Eventually, I discovered that I was running out of paper, and when I glanced at my digital clock, I was shocked to see it was already 2:33 in the afternoon. I hadn't budged from my desk in several hours!

Stiff and hungry, I decided it was time to take a break. I would see what I could find downstairs to nibble, and then I would go out to the stationery store for more paper.

Gram had left some cheddar cheese in our nearly bare refrigerator, so I took a mouthful before putting on my down jacket, hat, and gloves. Locking the door behind me, I headed downtown. The temperature must have dropped twenty degrees since the morning, because I could see my breath in front of me as I walked, and the gray sky looked ominously like snow.

When I finally got to the toasty warm stationery store with its frosted windows, I bought paper clips, a felt tip pen, and the January issue of *Seventeen*, just to make the trip worthwhile.

Outside, snow was falling heavily, and the cars, buildings, and sidewalk all looked sugar-coated. I crossed over to the other side so I could take a look in some different store windows on the way home. Walking along, paper bag under my arm, I enjoyed the sparkling Christmas displays as the falling snow chilled my face. Up ahead was a wooden bench set back from the sidewalk in a little grassy area. In warm weather, it was a nice place to rest and watch the downtown activity. In the cold snow, it was the last place I would want to sit.

Getting closer to the bench I happened to notice that there was a person sitting on it bundled in a huge navy parka, navy ski cap, jeans, and work boots. It was a remotely familiar figure too, and as I came nearer I realized exactly who it was.

"Sandy Moore, are you nuts?" I demanded, startling him out of his concentration. "You're going to get frostbitten." He looked at me a moment until recognition set in.

"Come on," he said, sounding annoyed. "It's not that cold."

"Feels like thirty below to me."

"Baloney."

"What are you doing out here, anyway?"

"What does it look like?" He held forward his sketchbook so I could see the beautiful rendering he was doing in pen of the row of small shops across the street, one being the stationery store I had just left. "I was in the mood for a little architecture," he explained.

"You certainly picked the right weather."

"The cold doesn't bother me, but now that it's snowing I'm going to have to stop. The ink is smearing." He blotted the page with a tissue from his pocket and closed the book. "Besides," he continued, stowing the sketchbook in the olive-green knapsack by his side, "I needed to get out of the house for a while. My cousins are visiting from Utah, three of them under five, if you can imagine, and it was getting a little intense."

"You should come to my house," I said, then laughed. "My whole family's away."

"Yeh? How'd you work that?" I gave him a brief rundown of the complicated arrangements. "What a deal," he commented when I was done. "My folks never go away for long. They're too busy working here."

"Don't they ever take vacations?"

"That's a laugh. They're workaholics, and it's

nearly impossible to get them to stop for more than a day or two. Of course, they go away to conventions and meetings every now and then, but only for a few days at a time."

"What do they do?" I asked, wondering if I had the right. Sandy was being so much more communicative than he'd ever been before, and I didn't want to put him off with embarrassing questions. I know how it upsets me when a stranger asks about my parents.

"They're in journalism," Sandy told me. "The *North Hollow Herald* is theirs."

"Whew," I whistled. The *Herald* was a paper to respect.

"Yes," he continued, "and I really can't knock it. Dad's head of editorial and Mom's the business manager. It's just that it's such a day-and-night thing. But then, isn't that true of anything that's worthwhile?"

"I don't know," I told him honestly. "It does seem that things worth doing are usually hard work, but whether it has to be day and night, I'm not sure."

"Well, for them it is, anyway."

"Hey, have they ever printed any of your drawings?" I asked brightly, seeing the paper as an obvious showcase for Sandy's work.

"They have offered," he acknowledged, "but I couldn't stand it if somebody said my work was lousy and the only reason it was in the *Herald* was because I was the son of the owners."

"But your drawings are terrific."

"Thanks, but I'm determined to make it on my own. . . . Well, I think I'll head home now," he announced in the next breath, threatening to end the longest conversation we had ever had together. "Which way are you going?" he asked as an after-thought.

"Down to Cheshire Drive."

"Oh yeh? That's the way I'm heading. I'm on Hartwick. It's not far from there. Do you know it?"

"My best friend used to live at 44."

"The stucco house with the blue shutters?"

"Yes. Did you know the Kramers?"

"No, but I drew the house a lot. I really love those arches, the great windows, and the fantastic red tile roof. We're at 59, across the street. It's an okay house, but pretty usual. It's white clapboard outside, with black shutters, and shaped like a box."

"Hey, it sounds a lot like my house, except mine is stone outside. That style has a funny name."

"Yes, a center-hall Colonial, and there were a lot of them built around here about fifty years ago. Ours has a great third floor that I've taken over as my workshop. My mother has even given me permission to kick out my little brother anytime he starts to bother me. I love it."

"We have a third floor, too, but my folks have their studios up there." Not wanting to discuss my parents any further, I hurried on. "So why were you sitting in the cold today, if you have your own private place?"

"Oh, everyone expects me to be sociable when we have the family visiting. They only come once a year. The only way I could get out of it was to leave the house altogether." Walking as briskly as the slushy streets would allow, we were nearing the turn to my street.

"Here's Cheshire," I announced to Sandy, wishing very much that we had another mile to go. "My house is another block down."

"See ya," he told me without further conversation.

"See you in study hall," I called after him, but he was already gone.

That was a weird experience, to be sure, and later that night, when Susan asked me about my day, I told her I had met and actually had a conversation with Sandy Moore.

"So what's he like?" She wanted to know.

"You tell me," I responded. "He was sitting out in the snow drawing."

"Bananas," she concluded.

"Just what I've said all along," I agreed. I would rather have met Tim out on my walk, but that was something I couldn't tell Susan.

The next day there was two feet of snow on the ground, and Susan had another date with Matthew. They were going to see *The Lady Vanishes*.

"What a novel idea," I observed.

"Yes, would you like to join us since you didn't get there yesterday?"

"It's nice of you to ask, but I think I'd rather work on something at home that I started yesterday morning."

"Oh, what's that?" she asked.

I told her about my story. "It's really in the beginning stages," I concluded, "but I've been thinking about it all night, and I'm dying to get back to work."

7

The last Sunday morning before school started, when the story was nearly finished, Mom and Dad arrived home exhausted form their tour. A few hours later, Gram and Jonathan arrived, enviably tan.

With everybody home, life suddenly became familiar again, almost as if they had never been away. Except, something had changed inside of me. On the verge of finishing my first, really important short story, a project that had engrossed me the way nothing else ever had, I was filled with a new feeling of confidence about myself. The story had dominated my thoughts so completely that I hardly had time to think about anything else, not even Tim.

Now with my family home and school about to start, he came back to my mind bigger and stronger than ever before. The end of Christmas vacation held special promise for me. I knew Tim's booster club fund drive would be beginning. I had tried joining other school activities and been driven away by my own fears. This time I was determined to let nothing stop me.

Monday, the first day back, was one of those days when nothing much got done. Classes were especially dull, and I didn't see Tim anywhere in the hall, which was a great disappointment. In study hall, Sandy would hardly communicate, keeping his head buried in some science fiction book with brightly colored planets on the cover.

Tuesday was assembly day, and after Mr. Hollingsworth made several boring announcements, there was Tim, at long last, standing on stage announcing the beginning of the booster club fund drive, just as he'd promised so many weeks ago.

"And I'd like to introduce you to the chairperson of our fund drive, a super cheerleader and a super girl, Robin Michaels," raved Tim with the confidence of a professional. The girl I had seen practicing with Laurel came forward wearing a gray pleated skirt and her black cheerleading sweater with a big red "N."

Robin gave everyone a big, glossy smile and waved. I expected her to make a pitch for the booster club, but instead Tim continued: "Robin and I will be in the booster office in room 301B right after assembly and every eighth period this week. We're hoping you'll drop in to sign up for our great winter fund drive. All we need you to do is to take orders for delicious oranges and grapefruit, which will be coming all the way from sunny Florida. The student government stands to make thousands of dollars with your help, so please come on in to pick up your instruction sheets and order forms."

As soon as assembly let out, I headed to room 301B. Tim would be there, and I could hardly wait. There were so many people milling around waiting to sign up that I was proud of Tim as he stood in the middle of it all. But he and Robin were surrounded by such crowds that it was impossible to get through to either of them. Suddenly Tim's voice cut across the chaos, and everyone stopped to listen. "May I have your attention please," he asked the group. "There are order forms in this carton and instruction sheets on the table; take one of each and sign your name, phone number, and grade. All orders must be in by January twentieth at the latest—that's three weeks from now. Get them in as soon as you get them so we can see how we're doing. Be sure to get payment in advance; checks are okay, and prices are listed on the instruction sheets. Thank you, ahead of time, for your help, and if there are any special questions you have, wait and ask me or Robin." With that, his announcement was over, and I went forward to pick up the materials he had described.

Reading through the instructions, I found everything clearly explained. I could leave without a word and start selling fruit. But I was still feeling bold. I waited around for the crowd to thin, determined to have a few words with Tim.

Would he remember me? I wondered. After all, the only time we ever met was months ago at my parents' dinner party.

As it turned out, in only a few minutes, Tim saw me and came over.

"Hi," he said in his wonderful, friendly way. "Bonnie, isn't it?"

"Barbara," I corrected.

"Oh, that's right," he picked up. "Barbara Lane."

"Right. I just wanted to see if there was anything else I could do besides take orders. I *am* intending to sell fruit, of course," I added hurriedly, "but just in case you need anything else done, I wanted to say I'm available."

"That's great, Barbara, and we really appreciate it, but at this point, taking orders is the big thing. Let me introduce you to Robin. She'll be doing all the bookkeeping." He waited until it looked like her conversation had ended with the girl she was talking to. "Robin, this is my friend Barbara Lane who wants to volunteer extra time. She may turn out to be very useful, and I just know you two will hit it off. Barbara, thanks for coming." With that, Tim turned to speak to a short, stocky boy who had been waiting by his side.

"Well, hi," Robin greeted in a voice that was startling in its nasal vagueness. "So you're an old friend of Tim's." It was hard to believe this person was a cheerleader.

"What was it you had in mind to do?" she asked in a condescending tone.

"Surely you must need help."

"Not really. Just get lots and lots of fruit orders and get your friends to do it, too. Hit up your family and neighbors, anybody nearby."

"No problem," I assured her.

I went home and sold three dozen oranges and a dozen grapefruits to my grandmother, had dinner, and went upstairs to finish re-typing the last few pages of my story.

When it was finally done and proofread, I put it in a manila envelope, picked up my fruit order forms, and went next door. The Hanovers always ate dinner late, although I found only Susan and her mother left at the table having dessert.

"Barbara, how nice to see you," greeted Mrs. Hanover.

"What have you got there?" Susan wanted to know.

"Actually, it's an order pad for the student government citrus sale. Would you guys like to buy some oranges and grapefruit?" I asked. "It's for a very good cause."

"Oh pooh," said Susan, giving real support to my sales pitch. "I'm going upstairs, Barbara; come on up when you're done."

"Tell me about the cause," said Mrs. Hanover kindly, and when I was done she ordered a dozen oranges and six grapefruits.

"I can't believe you're really doing this," scoffed Susan when I went upstairs.

"Why not? It's fun, and the fruit is supposed to be delicious. Besides, you told me months ago that I should get out and do something. This seemed like a good thing."

"I can't believe you take that nerd Tim Halpern so seriously." When she abruptly changed the subject, I was relieved.

"So what else do you have there? What's in that other envelope?"

"It's my story," I said shyly. "I just finished it."

"No kidding! That's great. Can I read it?"

"Are you sure you want to? You're not just being nice?"

"No, I really want to. I'm dying to find out what took up your entire Christmas vacation."

"If you're sure, then I'll leave it here for you."

"Terrific, and I'll give it back tomorrow morning on the way to school—unless you want it tonight."

"Tomorrow's fine," I answered. "See ya!"

"Hey, Barbara, I really liked this thing," Susan told me as she handed me back the manila envelope the next morning, "especially when Beth goes to school for the first time. It was a lot like I felt last year when we moved here. And I really like the way you wrote it, diary style. So what are you going to do with it now?"

Susan may have prefered calculators to typewriters, but she was smart, and I really respected her opinion. "I'll probably just put it in my drawer and forget it." I said.

"That's stupid. Why don't you at least show it to your English teacher or submit it to the school paper. They print short stories in the literary supplement, don't they?"

I could only shake my head and wriggle my nose. "Thanks for the show of confidence, but there's something you're forgetting, I think."

"What's that?"

"Who's my English teacher, and who's the faculty advisor to the school paper?"

"Rush?"

"Right."

"So I thought things were a lot better for you this year."

"Better means he's stopped picking on me, but it doesn't mean he treats me like a normal student."

"Barbara, what *are* you talking about? I never

understood what the big deal is between you and him."

"I really can't stand talking about it."

"Great, then how am I *ever* going to understand?"

"I've never told anyone, except Jennifer," I confessed. "Do you promise not to tell a soul?"

"Of course, but is it that bad? Listen, if you can't tell, you can't; but maybe you'll feel better if you do."

"You're right, but it is a long story."

"So, we'll walk slowly; we're a little early this morning anyway."

I told Susan the whole sordid mess, and when I was done she whistled. "Whew, what a louse," she said. "But I still can't understand why you never said anything to your parents."

"The thing is that they wouldn't have understood at all. Their solution would have been to offer to look at Rush's songs, and that has always been the last thing I wanted."

"Don't you think that's being a little selfish?" she asked gently.

"Listen, Susan," I defended. "Suppose I wanted to be a textile designer, and I asked you to introduce me to your mother—"

"You know I would."

"Yes, but if you realized I had been buttering you up for a few months specifically because I wanted an introduction—"

"That would make me pretty mad."

"And then, after you explained that you just didn't do things like that, for private reasons, I started doing awful things to you to try to bully you into it."

"That would make me furious," she conceded.

"See what I mean." I sighed, having made my point. "Rush just made the thing get worse and worse. I can't help thinking it might have been different somehow if he hadn't been so obnoxious." I was sniffing, and my eyes stung.

"I never really realized," apologized Susan. "Barbara, you can't let him get away with this. It's such a waste. Why don't you at least submit the story to the literary supplement. Maybe he'll never see it."

"Yeh, but maybe he will. It would drive me up a wall if they took it and he killed it at the last moment. He'd do it too, I have no doubts, if he knew it was my story." We walked in silence for a little as I seethed inside. "Of course," I cried out suddenly, "if he didn't know it was mine, maybe there wouldn't be a problem. Maybe I'll hand in my story, but I won't use my own name."

"You're kidding."

"No, I'm perfectly serious."

"Whose name will you use?"

"I don't know. I think I'll just make up a brand new name, a nom de plume."

"You're nuts." Susan laughed. "Rush will figure it out eventually."

"Just as long as my story gets printed first, I don't mind. Now, this is all contingent upon its getting accepted. You're sure you like it?" I asked, needing more reassurance.

"Yes, I really do," she promised. "I read it twice, and I even showed it to Mom. And she liked it, too. I hope you don't mind."

"No, I'm flattered. At least I have a fighting

chance. Now want to help me think of a good name? It should be fun."

By the time we got to school that morning I had become Bonnie Street. Although Susan and I giggled over my new name, having a new identity made me feel mysterious and sophisticated.

During study hall, I wrote Bonnie Street, Sophomore, on top of my story, which I had already named (ironically, I thought) "New Girl in Town." The outside of the manila envelope I addressed to the editor of the school's literary supplement, Lynn Gardner. I had taken her name out of the current issue of the *Clarion*, which was stored in my locker.

I had my fruit sale envelope with me, too, the outside decorated with brightly colored press-on stickers of oranges that I had bought at the stationery store. They added a nice touch.

"Selling fruit?" wrote Sandy on a sheet of notebook paper, which he expertly slipped on my desk. Included was a drawing of a cherubic little girl wearing a grass skirt and a bowl full of oranges on her head, who looked very much like the logo on our orange juice container at home.

"Don't worry," I told him on the same paper. "I already put through your order for a crate of oranges."

"All this so North Hollow can buy a new football?" he wrote back.

"Sour grapes," I scribbled.

"Very funny," he answered, and we both smiled at my fruit joke. That he didn't seem to notice the other manila envelope I had with me was a relief. I was planning to tell Sandy what I had done once it had been accomplished. If I failed, he need never know.

Our correspondence ended when Sandy got involved drawing in his sketchbook, and it took great self-control for me not to pull out my story and re-read it for the hundredth time, just to make sure everything was right.

Instead, I squirmed my way through geometry and history classes, and when the lunch bell finally rang, I ran downstairs to the newspaper office to slip the envelope through the mail slot before someone arrived to see me. I was determined to remain anonymous for the time being.

I sat with Jane at lunch; but too nervous to do anything but pick at my food, I hardly said a word. Susan passed by with Matt, each carrying a big brown lunch tray. "Did you do it?" she whispered conspiratorially, coming up behind my chair.

"Fait accompli," I told her, making a circle with my thumb and forefinger, glad to use a little something from French class.

Even though I knew it was too soon, I studied Mr. Rush closely during English class next period. One part of me irrationally expected that he had read and loved my story in the hour since I had deposited it in the newspaper office. But instead, he just paced around our classroom in his usual style, trying to stir up discussion about Julius Caesar. The class, as a group, resisted all his efforts at stimulation, and I could see his frustration quietly turning to rage. What a relief it was for everyone when the bell finally rang.

By the time classes were over for the day, the growing expectation of seeing Tim had filled my

mind so completely that I was able to forget about
my story for a while. I headed back downstairs to the
booster office with my other envelope, eager to show
off my first day's sales. The door to Room 301B was
locked, to my frustration; but since I planned to
make a lot more sales, I stuck my completed order
forms and checks in the mail slot, intending that
Tim, when he finally did arrive, would find them and
think of me.

Climbing upstairs and heading for my locker, I
passed Mrs. Squire, my guidance counselor, whom I
had hardly seen since the beginning of school.

"Hi, Barbara," she greeted with a warm smile.
"How are things going? Any better?"

We chatted for a few minutes, and Mrs. Squire
gave me a very nice order, part of which, she told
me, was for her grown son and daughter who lived
nearby. Our business completed, I continued down
the hall to my locker.

As I stood twirling the dial of my combination
lock, I heard the noise of rushing feet. Looking up, I
was surprised to see Robin, her usual glamorous
self, clicking down the hall in a pair of high-heeled
cowboy boots. Her hair, swept up high into an
off-center ponytail, was falling down in all the right
places.

"Hi," she greeted in her peculiar nasal voice as
she rushed on.

"I left some orders in the booster office," I yelled
after her.

"Oh," she said, stopping for a moment as if
startled by my information. "Thanks a lot." Then
she continued down the hall without another word.

Robin's stylish image stayed clear in my mind as I

slammed my locker shut, put on my warm winter jacket, and gathered my books. She must be rushing downstairs to the office, I told myself, even though I knew she was headed in the wrong direction for that. But as I neared the main door on my way out, whom should I see sitting on a wooden bench—smiling, giggling, her hurry very much forgotten? It was Robin, and she wasn't alone either.

Sitting next to her, much closer than necessary, was Tim. I don't know what they were saying to each other, but whatever it was, it didn't look like business.

I felt as if I were looking at them through a keyhole. They didn't notice me, I'm glad to say, and when Tim put his arm around Robin's shoulders and gave her a squeeze, I felt distinctly ill.

My fury, as I steamed home, was so great that I hardly noticed the freezing air. So Robin Michaels was Tim's type! I should have known he went for glamorous, overstated looks. Although she was pleasant-looking, Robin's features, up close, seemed to me to be outright ugly. But she did have a great figure, and the more I studied her, the more I realized it was the way she dressed herself that made her stand out and look so attractive.

I had been thinking that glamour was the way to go, but I never had the nerve to follow through on my instinct. I was pretty enough, and I had a reasonable figure, but it was subtle. Now there would be no more messing around. After all, I had a glamorous mother who was willing and able to help me. All I needed was the guts to follow her suggestions.

*   *   *

Mom wasn't home when I got there, just Gram. "I expect them back around seven o'clock," Gram told me, "so dinner might be late. Have a snack if you're hungry." I went upstairs to polish off my homework, so I could leave the rest of the evening free.

I heard the commotion of my folks arrival at about seven fifteen. Starving, I dashed downstairs to eat.

Afterward, Dad disappeared up to his studio, Jonathan turned on the TV in the den, Gram sat down with a book in the living room, and Mom nursed a second cup of coffee in the dining room.

"Mom, I've got a favor," I said when I was sure no one else was around. "I could use a little help."

"Certainly, honey, what can I do for you?"

"Well, I am going to be fifteen soon, and I want to do a little something to look more grown-up."

"What did you have in mind?"

"Well, I have a lot of nice clothes you've been buying me, but I've never worn them because I feel like I need to do up the rest of myself differently— things like changing my hairstyle and even wearing a little makeup. Do you think you could give me some advice?"

"Of course, honey. If you give me another five minutes to gather my strength, we can do a little something now."

"For real? You're not too wiped out?"

"No, I'm fine. What about your homework?"

"I did it this afternoon."

"Then meet me in my room with your brush in about five minutes. Do you still have those jars of makeup we bought?"

"Yes, but I need you to show me again how to use them," I apologized.

"No problem, honey. It just takes practice."

Mom and I had a great time. We started with makeup that she thought was more basic.

"Let me do a full daytime number first, and then you can decide how elaborate you want to get."

I gave her the jars she had bought me, but that I had only used once, and she looked them over carefully.

Mom began on my face, explaining as she went: "Always cleanse and moisturize first," she said, as she wiped my face with astringent on a cotton ball. Then an aloe cream. "Now, begin applying cover-up around the inside of the eye and down the nose. Better too little than too much," she warned as she blended it with her fingers, "or you'll look like a painted lady. Now have a look. What do you think?"

My face felt as though it weighed five hundred pounds, but I was willing to endure that for the time being. "I can't believe it's me. I love it. I really look grown-up."

"That you do," she confirmed, "and very pretty."

"Thanks Mom, and now if you can show me again so I can do it myself—"

"Fine. Let's start again. I'll do half of your face, and you can do the other" she said. "Here's the cleanser; take everything off."

On the back of an envelope, she drew a silly little sketch of my face with numbers and arrows that I could use as a reminder for myself. Next to it, she scrawled a list of what I should do and in what order.

"Mom, If I leave off the eye shadow for school,

will it ruin the whole thing? I just think it's a little much for everyday wear."

"I agree completely," she said. "Save the shadow for special occasions." She experimented with a few hairstyles: one side pulled over the top of my head and clipped, a high ponytail (like Robin's!), two braids pulled back at the sides. It was fun, but Mom was definitely better at doing it than I.

"It takes time and practice," she assured me.

"But I'm always so rushed in the morning!"

"Here's one that takes no time at all." She pushed my hair down and fastened one side back with a clip. "See, it takes about two seconds. Now you try it." She removed the clip.

"Good," she told me when I had done it myself, "now the next time, put the clip just a bit higher, like here." She touched the side of my head gently.

I tried it once more, and she gave her approval. "That's it for tonight, honey, I'm really pooped. But you look great. Wash your face well, moisturize it, and go to bed." It was eleven thirty, and I needed no prodding.

I had no trouble falling asleep, and when I woke up earlier than usual the next morning, I knew I had been practicing my makeup all night in my dreams.

Getting ready for school, I put on a fuzzy magenta turtleneck sweater (from Mom), a practically new pair of tight designer jeans, and pointy high-heeled boots that I had owned since last winter but had never worn. I combed my hair back to one side, as Mom had suggested, and carefully put on my make-up, glad to have her scrawly sketch and list to remind me what to do. As it took more than an hour to get ready, I was glad I had gotten up early.

8

You look so glamorous," Jane told me in school that Thursday, her voice filled with envy.

"Thanks Jane, I'm trying to turn over a new leaf. My mother helped me with my hair and makeup, but if you want to know the truth, I feel that if I smile, my face will crack."

"You'll get used to it, I'm sure, and one day," she had suddenly become embarrassed, "would you show me how to do it?"

"Of course," I promised, "but I'm not your ideal teacher, you realize. I hardly know what I'm doing myself."

Jane was the only one who said anything about the "new me," which was both disappointing and satisfying at the same time. Susan hadn't said a word, but maybe that was because having had a fight with Matt, she was immersed in her own private misery. Still and all, I liked to think that I looked grown-up and sophisticated, not waxy and obvious.

* * *

Every morning that week I got up early, chose some daring new outfit from my overpacked closet, did my hair, and put on makeup. Jane was still my biggest fan, except for my mother (if mothers count when it comes to that stuff), but by the end of the week, I still hadn't gotten completely comfortable with the "new me."

Meantime, I secretly studied the newspaper-office bulletin board every day, waiting for some correspondence or other for Bonnie Street, but none arrived. Within a few days I was beginning to resign myself to failure, and it felt rotten!

But, the week wasn't a total disaster. I was turning out to be an ace fruit salesman. I had sold fruit to all our neighbors up and down Cheshire Drive and was amassing an impressive record. Not that I loved doing it, but knowing that each sale I made would give me an excuse to visit the booster office and maybe see Tim spurred me on to greater and greater heights.

When I went down to the booster office at the end of the week with my latest orders, I found Robin sitting at the big, battered desk fretfully leafing through a pile of orders. For once, she looked at loose ends.

"Wow, sales look good," I observed.

"Yeh, too good," she whined. "Now I've got to get all this stuff sorted and entered into the ledger. What a drag, and I'm going to be late for my appointment at the dermatologist!"

"If you want, I'd be glad to work on that stuff for a while," I offered.

"Well, uh,"—I could see her mind working—"I'm not sure if I should. Actually," she quickly reconsidered, "If you have half an hour, I'd really appreciate your help; then I could get to my doctor's appointment on time."

Robin showed me how to enter all the information from the order forms and record the checks.

"Now, leave the checks and a duplicate record sheet with Mrs. Hobbs at the main office; she's only there until five," she concluded, handing me the key to the booster office. "Oh dear, if you have the only key, it means you'll have to meet me here first thing eighth period tomorrow. Can you do it?" She sounded annoyed at the possible inconvenience.

"Sure."

"Don't be late," she warned, and then fled thanklessly down the hall.

I worked on the orders for nearly an hour, shocked to discover that none of my own had been recorded. In fact, there were only a few entries made at all, and I began to realize that after all this time, Robin had just barely begun to keep the books. I have to admit that the bookkeeping was terribly tedious, but it had to be done, and so I plowed my way through it.

As I worked, a few kids wandered in with more orders, a welcome distraction from the pages and pages of numbers. Meantime, I began wondering about Robin's curious behavior. She had been so busy turning down my offers of help, yet it was clear to me that she really needed it. What was going on here, anyway?

It had been a not particularly constructive afternoon as far as my real goals were concerned. But I did offer, after all, and while I was no math whiz, I had to admit that with my neat handwriting, I had made some very attractive lists.

By 4:30, the orders were finally recorded, and it was time to pack up before Mrs. Hobbs left the main office. Besides, I hadn't even begun my homework. As I surveyed the desk top, trying to decide if everything was organized to my satisfaction, I heard someone come in the door.

Oh bother, I thought to myself, I'm leaving these new orders for Robin. Turning to confront the newcomer, I was shocked to see Tim.

"Hi there, Barbara," he greeted, "Where's Robin?" His cheeks were flushed as if he had just come out of the cold, and he looked so handsome I could hardly speak.

"Uh, she had an appointment, so I offered to do some bookkeeping."

"That's nice. How are sales?"

"They seem awfully good to me, but then, I don't know what you were expecting. Have a look for yourself." I opened the ledger and handed it to him.

Tim flipped through the pages and gave me a big grin. "I'll say it looks great. Look at those gorgeous numbers, and I have a pile of more orders in my locker." Pulling out a tiny calculator from under his coat, he continued, "Read off the numbers to me will you? Let's get some idea of what we've got."

I began reading off the columns of numbers while Tim punched away at the tiny buttons. It took quite a while to get through all the pages, but when we were done, Tim was thrilled. "One thousand, four hundred, seventy-three dollars, and thirty-nine cents," he announced. "Of course, that's gross, but then, this is only the first week."

"What's your goal?" I asked.

"I'd like to net about $2,500. Do you think we can do it?"

"If this is any indication, I don't see why not. But that's an awful lot of oranges!"

"You're not kidding," he laughed.

"How is this thing going to work, exactly?"

"Once we have all the orders, we send a deposit to this place in Florida, and they ship the oranges and grapefruit up in a big truck C.O.D."

"Then what?"

"What do you mean?"

"How do people get their oranges and grape-fruits?"

"The salespeople will distribute them, of course."

"Good heavens, I've sold dozens and dozens. I never realized I was going to have to lug them all over the place."

Tim only laughed at my revelation, but I had an uncomfortable feeling that I wasn't going to be the only person who was going to need help.

Looking at my watch, I saw that it had gotten late. "Oh dear," I groaned, "it's 5:15 already, and Mrs. Hobbs will have left the main office. I was supposed to have given her the checks."

"Do it in the morning," Tim suggested. "Robin's been keeping them in her locker until now, anyway. Just be sure to turn them in first thing tomorrow so they can be deposited in our account. Well, I've got to be getting home. Need a ride?" he asked, in such a casual way that I couldn't believe what I had heard.

"Uh," I responded, "uh, sure, if it's not out of your way."

"Come on. Put away the checks, grab your stuff, and let's go."

Locking the door behind us, I walked upstairs with Tim Halpern at my side. As we headed out to the parking lot, I was overcome with euphoria. We walked in silence through the heavy front doors and onto the floodlit stone plaza. "I'm in the side lot," Tim said, motioning to the left. I followed along, hoping to come up with something brilliant to say.

Unlocking the side door on the passenger side of his small low car, he held it open for me. In the dark, it was hard to tell the color or make of the car, not that I would have known anyway, but it had an impressive dashboard cluttered with dials, buttons, and a stereo tape deck.

"Want to hear something?" he offered. "There are a bunch of tapes in the glove compartment."

"Sure," I agreed, but when I opened it up and tried to find something that I would consider appropriate mood music, I was stumped. In the low light from inside the glove compartment, I saw only tapes of groups like Kiss, Blondie, and The Rolling Stones. Finally, finding an old Beatles tape, I handed it to him. "Here's one I love," I told him.

"Fine," he agreed, without knowing what it was. "Is the West and Lane in there? I just bought their new album, but I'm not sure if it's in there yet."

The tape I had chosen was now filling the car with music, making conversation difficult.

"I really don't listen to their stuff much anymore," I admitted. "When I was younger it was exciting, but now I prefer other things. After all, they're my parents, and their music is too old, if you know what I mean."

We were driving away from school, and Tim, mostly looking into the red taillights ahead, was glancing into the rearview mirror every now and then. "That's silly," he condemned. "I think you just take them for granted because they're your folks."

"Maybe," I allowed.

We were at my house so quickly, I didn't have to pursue this subject any further. But, as Tim was pulling into the crescent driveway, I searched desperately for a way to prolong my time with him.

"Would you like to come in and say hello?" I suggested.

"No, thanks. I have to grab a bite at home and be back at school by 7:15 for basketball practice."

"I had no idea you practiced at night."

"We don't usually, but the all-county finals are coming up, and we really want to do well. Last year we missed getting into the all-state competition by one game, so this year we decided to put everything we have into a big win."

"When do you do homework, or student government stuff, for that matter?"

"That is a problem right now," he conceded, "but for the moment basketball is high priority."

"Good luck," I wished him, "and thanks for the ride."

"See you," he told me, "and thanks for the help with the booster club. Tell Robin I'll be in during eighth period with a big pile of orders."

"No problem," I replied, as I slammed the door and ran into the house.

Dad was sitting in the den wearing a beige cashmere cardigan over his white shirt. Smoking a pipe, with his feet up on the leather hassock, he looked very content.

"Hi, Barb," he greeted. "What's up?"

"Nothing much. Just some after school stuff keeping me busy."

"That's nice. You got a ride home, I take it, from the sound in the driveway."

"Yeh," I agreed, "someone from school."

"Oh?" His eyebrows went up as he looked at me over his reading glasses.

"His name is Tim," I mumbled, wondering if he would catch on.

"T.J.'s son?" he asked, his eyes lighting up.

"As a matter of fact, yes."

"Isn't that nice," he mused.

"Well, I've got to get rid of all this stuff," I announced, putting an end to our already too long conversation.

Upstairs, I thought back over every scrap of conversation Tim and I had exchanged. It hadn't gone exactly as I would have wanted, but it was still pretty good. His image was so clear in my mind, it was almost as if it were happening again.

I sat through dinner, still in a cloud, until I realized that Dad was spilling the beans to the rest of the family.

"And guess who gave our baby a ride home?" he said.

"I have no idea," said Mom.

"T.J.'s boy, Timmy."

"My, my," responded Mom, eyeing me with interest.

"Yes," I told her, dying inside, "I was helping out with the fund drive, and he gave me a ride home afterward."

"Well, I like to see you busy," approved Dad, "and I couldn't be more pleased with your beau if I had chosen him myself."

Family, family, family, I raged inside. Whoever invented them was a lunatic! What right did anyone here have to question me about my social life? And the nerve of Dad to assume that just because Tim Halpern drove me home from school once, he was my boyfriend! It was outrageous! It was disgusting! It was infuriating! He was so completely wrong. The awful part was that I so much wanted Dad to be right.

The next morning, I dressed carefully in a brown corduroy jean skirt and a pink shirt and sweater and refreshed my makeup and hair like an old pro in the girls' room during lunch. Feeling that I looked good, I was ready for anything, and my mind was focusing in and out on what might happen during eighth period.

My arrival downstairs at the booster office seemed somehow important. As it turned out, Robin was nearly ten minutes late. Gliding in the door, she looked gorgeous, as usual. "Hi," she droned through her nose. "Glad to see you're here." More orders had been stuck through the mail slot during the day, and I was busy doing the paperwork.

"Did you get the checks to Mrs. Hobbs?" she asked, her voice businesslike.

"No, actually, it took longer than we thought, so I handed them in this morning. No problem."

"Didn't I tell you they had to be in last night?" she snarled.

"Tim said this morning would be okay," I assured her, suppressing my own irritation at her rude behavior. After all, I wasn't doing all this paperwork that was hanging around the office to be nice to her.

"Oh." That stopped her. "He was here?"

"Yes, and he was very pleased with the sales so far," I volunteered. "Want to have a look?" I handed her the opened ledger.

"Great," she said, hardly looking. "Did he ask for me?"

"Yes. I said you had an appointment."

"Thanks."

"There are some new orders, which I'm working on now. Do you want to finish up?" I started to move away from my place at the desk.

"Well, uh," she looked at her watch, "you might as well finish what you're doing, and I'll be back later on. If I'm not here by four, just lock up, and I'll get the key from you the same time tomorrow, if that's convenient."

"Fine, I'll see you later."

Starting to leave, she turned back suddenly. "Uh, one other thing."

"Yes?"

"What was your name again?"

"Barbara."

"Right. Well, thanks Barbara. See ya' around."

She swept out of the room, and I was glad I had neglected to tell her that I was expecting Tim to arrive at any moment. Glamorous Robin was turning out to be a creep.

It took me another twenty minutes to finish up the

orders I had, and still Tim hadn't arrived. It was nearly a quarter to four, and I was worrying that Robin might be back early. Actually, I was hoping she wouldn't be back at all. I wasn't ready to surrender the booster club key.

By the time Tim walked in at 4:20, I was closing up my geometry homework and gathering up the order forms and checks.

"Glad I caught you," Tim told me, and my heart lurched at the possible sentiment. "How's business today?"

"Have a look." I opened up the ledger and held it forward for him to see. "Everything from here down is new." It was déjà vu, and I was hoping that the afternoon would turn out the same as yesterday, but better.

"Very, very nice, and I have at least that much here." He handed me a battered interoffice envelope. "Where's Robin?"

"I'm not sure where she went, but she said she might be coming back," I told him, hoping to be vague in my honesty.

"How about if I read off my orders to you so you can get them into the ledger book. It'll be faster that way. Maybe we'll have time to get the checks to Mrs. Hobbs. Do you have time now?"

"Sure, let's get it out of the way," I said, attempting to be casual. Inside, my heart was beating fast.

Tim pulled up a big old wooden chair, and we got to work. This progressed nicely for about ten minutes until Robin arrived, breathless and beautiful.

"Sorry to be late," she apologized meekly. "How do you like business so far?" she asked him, artfully batting her eyelashes.

"Looks just terrific," he confirmed. "You're doing just a bang-up job."

"Well, I try," she responded in her clever, demure little way. Silently, I seethed at the praise Tim had given to Robin, praise that should have been mine; but an inner voice told me to keep my cool. When he figured out who was doing all the work, my deeds would seem all the more glorious.

"Well, what's left to do?" she asked eagerly.

"Just a handful of orders. Barbara and I have been working on them."

"Fine. Thank you Barbara," she told me, "but I'm here now, and I'll finish up with Tim. Be sure to leave me the key, will you."

I flashed with anger at her dismissal, until I was hit with a revelation that made me jump eagerly from the chair. "Sure, Robin. Here's the book, here's the key. I've got to get going anyway. Bye, you guys."

Ordinarily, leaving them together would be something I would have tried to prevent at all costs, except for one important thing. So far, Robin had entered about four orders in the ledger out of the couple of hundred that were now there. When Tim saw Robin's back-slanted handwriting following pages and pages of my own clear printing, he'd have to know the truth.

On the way down the hall, I took another glance at the *Clarion*'s bulletin board, just in case there had been some last-minute mail for Bonnie Street, but there wasn't. I had handed in my story on Wednesday, and it was only Friday afternoon. But so much had happened since then, it seemed like a year ago.

But thoughts of my story faded from my mind as I wandered home in the near dark, reviewing what I had done in the booster office. I had left Robin there, alone with Tim, on purpose. Was I nuts? Although it seemed like a brilliant idea at the time, I was now having second thoughts. Should I rush back and see what was going on? I wondered. I could pretend I had left something in there. No, I resolved. What's done is done.

I thought about Tim all weekend, as I expanded my fruit-selling territory. Between Saturday and Sunday, I hit every house on the block and two blocks past. For the most part, people were very receptive, and my envelope was stuffed with completed order forms and checks and some cash.

The next street over was Jennifer's old block, Hartwick, and I found myself standing in front of her former house. Ringing the bell, I was relieved when no one answered the door.

Walking down the block, I made a few more sales, though nothing stupendous. When I got to the end, I crossed over to head back down the other side. It was a pretty block, a lot like my own, with big sprawling houses set back on large, well-tended lawns.

Suddenly, I was standing in front of a house with the same pretty glass fan-window over the front door as we had on our house. Looking harder, I realized that it must be Sandy Moore's house. Since I knew for sure that Sandy had no interest in selling fruit for the fund drive, I had no compunction about seeing if anyone else in his family might want to place an order with me.

Sandy had said his folks were hardly ever home, but it was Saturday, so maybe one of them would be there. If Sandy answered the door, would he laugh me out of the house, I wondered.

Resolved to make a sale, I rang the bell. A thin woman in casual slacks and a neat cashmere sweater answered. Despite her nicely styled hair tinged with gray, which was so different from Sandy's usual disarray, she looked as though she might be his mother.

"Yes?" she asked pleasantly.

"Hi, I'm Barbara Lane. I live over on Cheshire, and I'm selling oranges and grapefruit for the high school fund drive. Do you think you might like to place an order?"

"Come in, come in," she invited.

I stepped inside as she closed the glossy black front door. Looking around, I couldn't believe my eyes. "Are you Sandy's mother?" I asked, unable to contain my mirth. The slated vestibule with the carved wooden staircase, the den, visible through the doorway, with its huge built-in bookcases and a fireplace all seemed so familiar. Even the comfortable but well-worn furniture that was in my field of vision, although not identical, was reminiscent of my parents' homey furnishings. And everywhere I looked, I saw another cat!

"Yes, are you a friend of his?" she asked.

"We know each other a little bit from school, and once, a long time ago, we were discussing houses—"

"Yes, Sandy loves old houses."

We chatted for a few minutes, and Sandy's mother ordered a few dozen oranges and half a dozen grapefruits.

"We love fresh-squeezed juice around here. I'm

surprised Sandy didn't tell me about the sale," she said, as I wrote up the order.

"He's not much into student government stuff," I apologized, as if I needed to make his excuses.

"It does make sense, you know," she said with regret. "His older brother, Ron, was president of North Hollow High when he was there some years back—very devoted he was, too. Ron's now at Harvard Law. A hard act to follow, I should imagine."

"It isn't as if Sandy doesn't have other interests," I said, falling deeper into conversation about Sandy with his very own mother.

"Yes, Sandy is a terrifically talented artist, but he's a shy boy and can be so stubborn about accepting help. Again, he's so different from Ron, who's always been so eager to get ahead. Of course, Sandy is very determined, and that, I'm sure, will serve him well in years to come."

Talking with Sandy's mother was an unexpected treat, and when I finally left, it was with the feeling that I had made a new friend.

"I hear my mother's mortgaging the house to buy oranges from you," Sandy wrote in a note on Monday morning in study hall.

"You'll never regret it," I answered back. "By the way, I almost dropped my teeth when I walked into your house. The inside is practically identical to mine, except you have more cats." I filled the scrap paper with neat printing as I enumerated all the similarities I could detect in the front vestibule and den alone. "Anyway," I continued in my note, "your Mom is really great."

"Yeh, actually she's okay," he conceded to my

surprise, "and she liked you, too." It felt good to know that Mrs. Moore had mentioned me to Sāndy, but I dared not let him in on the details of our conversation. Somehow, it seemed better to keep it to myself.

I had been waiting all weekend for a rematch with Robin and another chance to spend time with Tim, but when I got downstairs during eighth period, the booster office was locked with no sign of Robin anywhere.

Holding fast to my orders rather than putting them through the mail slot, I considered how best to use them to advance my friendship with Tim. I also wondered again what had happened after I had left them together on Friday afternoon. It was frustrating not to have any hint at all, especially after waiting so eagerly all day for eighth period.

Walking away from the locked booster office, I decided to wander down the hall a little more for a look at the *Clarion*'s bulletin board. The door was open, and as I passed it, I saw a few kids working at desks.

Just past the door was the bulletin board, which was covered with typewritten information sheets and five or six little envelopes that hadn't been there on Friday. Scanning the board, my eyes made a short stop when they saw Bonnie Street typed on one.

My body tensed as I looked up and down the hall. No one visible, I reached up and removed the note. Looking around again, I threw the envelope into my bag. How I longed to rip it open, but I knew that if the news was good, I'd need to hold on to my secret a little longer. If the news was bad, I might want to keep my secret forever.

Rushing down the hall and up the stairs, my footsteps echoing behind me, I headed for the privacy of the first-floor girls' room. It was empty, as I had hoped, but just to insure my privacy, I locked myself in one of the stalls before reaching for the note.

Tearing it open, I was thrilled to read, "To Bonnie Street: Your story, 'New Girl in Town,' has been selected for publication in the spring literary supplement of the North Hollow *Clarion*. Thank you for your submission, Lynn Gardner, editor." I breathed a sigh of relief, and tears came to my eyes as I realized what I had accomplished. I had written a story that was going to be printed in the school paper, the literary supplement at that! I tucked the note safely into my bag, ran to my locker to get my books and jacket, and practically flew home through the chilly afternoon air.

I wanted desperately to share my excitement, and there were only two people I could think of who would really appreciate my feat with all its implications. One was Susan, because she had been with me through so many steps of the struggle. The other person was (and it was weird to admit this to myself) Sandy Moore! He knew what it was like to be an unwilling victim of Mr. Rush, and he appreciated the value of succeeding at something all by oneself.

Susan had been complaining of a toothache that morning on the way to school, and I wondered how she was feeling now that it was late afternoon. Somehow I had missed her in the cafeteria during lunch.

Knocking quietly on the kitchen door, I was greeted by Mrs. Hanover. "Susan's upstairs feeling miserable because she has to have a wisdom tooth pulled tomorrow," she told me. "Maybe you can cheer her up."

I ran upstairs to find Susan lying on her side in bed. "It's me, Barbara. Are you okay? Your Mom told me about the tooth."

"Yeh, the dentist promised I wouldn't feel a thing. Easy for him to say! Barbara, it hurts so much, and I'm the world's worst chicken."

"Want me to come with you and hold your hand?"

"Thanks for the offer. Mom's promised though. She's even going to sleep early tonight so she can get up in time."

"Hey listen, I have good news, not that it's going to make your tooth any better."

"What's that?"

"Bonnie Street had her story accepted by the *Clarion*'s literary supplement."

"Hey, no kidding! That's great." Her face flushed with pleasure. I filled her in on the details, and though I knew she was excited for me, her responses were getting groggier and groggier.

"Dr. Minton gave me something for the pain," she mumbled, her eyes flickering.

"Good luck tomorrow morning," I whispered as I got up to leave, "and if you change your mind about my coming along, just give me a ring." But Susan didn't hear me because she had drifted off to sleep.

During dinner that night, I was dying to tell my family about the success of my story. But as excited as I was, I didn't know how I would explain my pseudonym to them without having to go into uncomfortable detail, so I ended up saying nothing.

By the end of dinner, I was bursting with such

excitement that I knew I had to tell someone. Sandy was the logical person, but I didn't think I could wait until morning.

Gazing at my French homework, twiddling my pen between my two fingers (as Sandy often did), I decided to be really daring. What could I lose by calling him up? He was a friend, after all.

I ran down to the kitchen and found his phone number in the slim little North Hollow directory.

Dialing the number back in the privacy of my own room, I was glad when he answered.

"Sandy, it's me Barbara."

"What's up?" he asked, his voice wary.

"I have the funniest thing to tell you," I started, feeling like maybe it had been a big mistake to call. "But it's a secret, okay?"

"Sure."

I told him my tale, and when I was done, I hoped he would echo my enthusiasm.

"I'm not sure if that's crazy or brilliant," he responded. "You realize what will happen if Rush catches on? He'll skin you alive."

"He need never know. You and my friend Susan are the only people I've told, and you guys are trustworthy. Once I get out of his class in June, there's nothing else he can do to me."

"Hey, what's he got against you anyway?"

"Well, uh," I hesitated, "that's kind of the biggest bummer of all. I really can't go into it."

"Have it your way," he allowed. "How are you doing these days with our favorite English teacher, anyway?"

"Just biding my time until June."

"What a waste. I've got Davis this year, and she is fantastic."

"Don't make me ill," I warned. "At least old Rush has let up his attack on me. That in itself is fantastic."

We talked more and more, and Sandy became so relaxed, it was like talking to an old friend. He had a nice sense of humor, and our conversation went on comfortably as we discovered how much we had in common.

We shared interests in things like old movies, animals (his family had five cats), and doing our own serious work, independent of school. For Sandy, it was his drawing; for me it was my journal and now my stories. While I was talking to him, I resolved to start another.

The only subject we hit upon that created instant friction was the North Hollow student government president, Tim Halpern, and his citrus fruit drive.

"You know, Barbara," he told me earnestly, "that guy is such a transparent jerk, I can't believe you still don't see it. Talk about useless."

"I think you're too hard on him," I replied. If I didn't know better, I might have accused him of being jealous. "He's no great political leader," I conceded, "but he's doing a decent job."

"Hmph," was all I got for a reply. "Well, see you in school."

9

I've been thinking all night about your secret," Sandy wrote in a note, which he slipped on my desk the next morning in study hall, "and I've decided that I'm definitely impressed."

"Thanks," I wrote back. "I'm glad to have your support. I was beginning to think no one cared." I hadn't seen Susan that morning, but I assumed she was on her way to the dentist.

"Don't be silly," he answered, "it just took me a while to realize what you have accomplished. So when can I read this great masterpiece?"

"I'd hardly call it that, and if that's what you are expecting, I'm going to be too embarrassed to show it to you," I sent back in a quick scrawl.

"Excuse me for the overstatement," he wrote. "I'm not expecting perfection, but I bet it's pretty good to be taken by the literary supplement. They don't print all that many long pieces."

"I guess you're right, not that I was thinking in

those terms exactly. For me, it just seemed like a good way to get involved with the paper despite you-know-who." I had started a new piece of paper.

"Great," he wrote underneath, "but how are you going to pull off anything else while you are still an alias?"

"I haven't worked out the details," I had to admit. "Meantime, what about you? Why don't you submit drawings to the paper? They always print artwork, and yours is so much better than anything they've ever had." Now that I was including Sandy in my own special secret, I never considered that he might object to my prying into his privacy, but I soon saw my mistake.

"Listen, I once told you that the high school rag was nothing to me. That you want to work on it is your own trip," he scrawled.

"Sorry, sorry," I wrote back quickly. I was afraid I had angered him to the point where he wouldn't even bother to reply, but instead, I was glad to see he was working on a drawing, which I hoped would be for me.

When he finally slipped it onto my desk, I saw that Sandy had depicted himself wearing huge sculptural wings, which he labeled "wax." Above him was a scowling, hot sun. "It might be a big mistake to fly so close," he had written underneath, and I knew I had interfered about as much as I could. Sandy was now hard at work on his math text, or at least he was putting on a pretty good show.

When the bell finally rang at the end of the period, I looked forward to exchanging a few face-to-face words with him, feeling that in the last day our friendship had grown tremendously. But as I began to make some cryptic remark about Bradshaw, I turned to see him making tracks out the door. I've really stuck my foot in my mouth this time, I scolded myself. But then, Sandy has always been a weirdo.

At lunch I looked around for Susan, but I didn't see her anywhere. Matt, however, was sitting alone at a table looking miserable. Whatever their disagreement had been, it was eating at both of them.

"Hi," I greeted him, "Susan was having a wisdom tooth pulled this morning, so I guess she's home recuperating."

"No kidding," he responded, his face showing sympathetic pain. "That's supposed to be a real bummer."

"Do you think she'd want to talk on the phone?" he asked shyly.

"I can't say exactly, but last night she seemed glad enough for the diversion."

"Then maybe I'll give her a call," he said, pushing himself away from the table, a smile spreading across his face. "Thanks, Barbara. See ya!"

At least I made someone feel good today, I congratulated myself. In fact, even though the pleasure I felt about having my story accepted and the anticipation of working with Tim burned stronger, Sandy's apparent rejection lurked at the back of my mind. I looked forward to eighth period when I could deliver my weekend sales downstairs.

But first I had to sit through our weekly assembly, with Mr. Hollingsworth making his boring announcements, not that I minded all that much. In the end, I would get to watch Tim while he made his announcements as student council president.

As always, he was wonderful, he was masterful, and my heart did flip-flops when he began to talk with pride about the fruit sale. "You guys are doing great things selling oranges and grapefruit, and we're already more than halfway to our goal. Keep up the good work! And just to celebrate our success, we'll be able to have a North Hollow winter dance, and everyone in the school is welcome. Come by yourself or with a date. It's definitely going to be the dance of the year, but meantime, be sure to keep bringing in those orders!"

Wouldn't it be wonderful to go to that dance with Tim! I closed my eyes for a moment as I pictured us together in the middle of the gym floor.

When assembly was over, I ran downstairs to see what was happening in the booster office. There was an impressive crowd gathered there clutching completed order forms and envelopes of money, and I said polite hellos to the familiar people who had handed in orders to me before.

Coming through the crush, Tim came over and put his arm gently on my arm. "Barbara," he beamed, "wait around, will you? There's something important I want to ask you."

How could I refuse a request like that? I stood there dazed as he floated back into the fray, making small talk with the students around me and answering any questions I could about the fruit sale. For the first time ever, I felt like I really belonged, and it felt great.

When the crowd began filtering out, leaving only Tim and Robin behind, I began wondering if Tim's question was public enough to be asked in front of her. As it turned out, Tim was anxious to see the new orders recorded and asked if one of us had the time to do it. He was ambiguous about whether he'd be staying around to work, and when Robin excused herself to go off to cheering practice, I was glad to volunteer.

"Aren't you going down to the gym to practice for the Greely game tomorrow?" she asked him as she stood by the door.

"Actually, I want to help Barbara get started," he explained. "I'll catch up."

"Okay, see ya!" she said with phony enthusiasm.

"Barbara, things are turning out better than I had even hoped," Tim told me when Robin had left, "and I know the bulk of the responsibility has fallen on you. I want you to know how much I appreciate it."

"I'm glad to do it."

"I was thinking how nice it would be to take you to the winter dance. Would you like to come with me?" Not believing what I had just heard, I stood there blinking like a fool.

"What do you think?" he persisted.

"Oh Tim, I'd love to go," I told him, breaking out of my reverie. "But what about Robin? I'm sure she's expecting to go with you." I made a little face.

"You know what? I think we'd better not tell her for a while. I wouldn't want it to interfere with your work together. At any rate, Bud Hollister is dying to invite her. He's my co-captain on the basketball team and a great guy."

"Fine."

"Meantime, I've got to get in an hour down at the

gym. Tomorrow's our important home game. You coming to it?"

"Sure, if I get these orders done in time," I laughed. The desk was piled with papers.

"Ah, Cinderella has to stay behind and do her work," he joked in a way I didn't much like. "But that's what I like about you," he told me, suddenly serious. "You've really been keeping on top of this stuff. Thanks a lot. I'll be going home around six thirty, so if you want a ride, drop by the gym."

"Thanks, but we usually eat dinner around then, and I've got a sick friend to visit."

"I'll look for you after the game tomorrow." He gave my arm a friendly squeeze.

"By the way, I don't have a key," I told him. "So be sure to drop by after practice and lock up."

"Barbara, I know you should have your own, but at the moment I don't want to antagonize Robin."

"Yeh," I agreed, knowing possession of the key wouldn't be the main issue.

When he left, I threw myself into the bookkeeping with greater devotion than ever before. Then I gathered up my books and headed home.

I went directly to Susan's house to see how she was doing, and when I rang her front door, she answered it herself.

"How was it? Are you okay?" I asked.

"It wasn't so-o-o bad," she confessed. "The best part is that it's over and all the pain is gone. And better than getting the tooth taken care of is that Matt called twice and we're going to be seeing each other again! We're going to do something special this weekend, and he was talking about some winter dance at school next week." She was radiant.

"I'm so glad," I told her. "I mentioned to Matt that you were sick when I saw him in the cafeteria at lunch."

"Barbara!"

"All I did was say you were having a tooth pulled! The calling part was completely his idea. But listen—" I continued in a different tone of voice, hoping to put an end to her scolding. "I've got a date for the winter dance, too."

"No kidding. Let me guess. That artist guy, Sandy what's-his-name?"

"Sandy Moore!" I was shocked at the thought. "Don't be silly. We'd have to spend the whole night writing notes to each other. No, my date is someone completely different, and are you ever in for a surprise!"

"I give up then."

"Tim Halpern."

"What!" She studied me with disbelief. "That jerk! I absolutely can't believe it. I know you thought he was cute and all, but from what I can see, you two have about as much in common as oil and water."

"Well, I should have known you'd say something revolting about my date. Tim Halpern, it so happens, is a really nice guy, and I'm thrilled to be going to the winter dance with him!"

"Have a good time," she told me, and furious, I went home.

As I marched up our front walk, I could see my mother through the frosted windows of the sun porch poking around the plants with a watering can.

"You look upset," she observed as I steamed in.

"Susan Hanover makes me so mad! I just got asked to the winter dance by a really neat guy, and Susan told me she thought he was a jerk!"

"That wasn't very nice."

"Well, she does have a way of saying what's on her mind. It never bothered me much before, but this time it makes me just furious."

"So, who's the guy?"

"Tim Halpern."

"Isn't that nice, dear." Though she carefully controlled her voice, I could tell she was delighted. "So our make-over work paid off."

"Yeh, I guess so." Somehow the truth was embarrassing.

"Your father will be so pleased."

"Do we have to tell him?" I was shocked.

"Why in heaven's name not?"

"You know Daddy. He gets so carried away."

"I'll ask him to keep it under his hat. How's that?"

"Thanks, but I wonder if he can."

I was so excited about going to the dance with Tim that for the next week and a half nothing could bother me: not Susan's sudden cold shoulder; not Sandy's apparent dislike of me (he stopped writing me notes in study hall altogether); not Robin's confrontation with me in the booster office about my date with Tim; not even Tim's insistence that he play a tape of my parents' hit single "Dreams" whenever he drove me home after school. Even the realization that my quest to get on the school paper might be stalemated left me unperturbed.

I did my homework diligently every night after working in the booster office. I even remembered to get my flowered dress to the dressmaker to have it altered in time to wear to the dance.

Finally the Big Night arrived.

"Let me see how my baby looks," demanded Dad as Mom put the finishing touches on my hair and makeup. Somehow his gushing enthusiasm made me feel about three years old. "Just glorious," he told me. "You must let me take your picture with Timmy later."

"Oh, Daddy," I groaned.

"Now, Marty," Mom objected, "this is only their first date, after all. Why don't you wait a while?"

"Daddy, I'm nervous enough as it is," I admitted, hoping he'd get the message.

"As you like, ladies," he finally capitulated.

But when the doorbell rang and Tim arrived, both my parents descended on him like vultures. He looked splendid in his immaculate khaki slacks, navy blazer, striped tie, and shiny loafers.

"Timmy Halpern," greeted Dad, pumping his hand, "How nice to see you again, son."

"Good to see you again too, Mr. Lane, Mrs. Lane."

"How's the old ball game?" Dad wanted to know immediately.

"Just fine; we're having a terrific season, as Barbara may have told you. We made the all-county finals, and we're hoping to go on to the big all-state playoffs in Albany." I nodded my head knowingly, although, to tell the truth, this was all news to me.

"Well, good going," congratulated Dad, giving Tim a too-familiar slap on the back. I was horrified, but Tim just beamed.

"And how's your fund drive going?" asked Mom.

"Just super," Tim confirmed, "but Barbara can tell you all about that. She's doing a tremendous job with the bookkeeping."

As Dad and Tim began talking about basketball again, Gram came in from the den and tapped me on the shoulder. "Come into the kitchen a moment," she said to me. "Tim, I'll bring her right back," she promised.

"You look just gorgeous," Gram told me in a soft voice when we were finally alone. "It brings tears to my eyes. Have a great time, but promise me you'll remember one important thing, and I'm saying this because I love you, Barbara. This may be your first big date, but it's also just the beginning. Tim is a dashing young man, but there's so much more to come."

"Oh Gram, you're silly," I said in equally hushed tones.

"No, I'm serious, Barbara. I don't want you to feel pressured by your parents' enthusiasm."

"Thanks, Gram," She gave me a warm hug, but I was unable to tell her that with or without my parents' blessings, Tim really was the boy of my dreams.

Tim and I finally got out of the house and drove the few blocks to school in Tim's familiar green car. He had pushed the button on his tape deck, and Mom and Dad's voices were coming out of the stereo speakers singing "Dreams." "I still can't understand why you don't listen to their music."

"I do like this one," I admitted.

The gym, decorated in white and silver, looked incredible. "Laurel and Joanne have been working on it since Friday night," Tim told me. "I'm glad you like it." The ceiling and walls were festooned with white streamers and masses of white helium-filled balloons. Suspended in the center of the ceiling was a giant silver mirrored ball, which sparkled in the low light as it slowly revolved. But best of all was the gym floor, which was covered with a dusting of silver glitter that was now clinging to everyone's legs and shoes.

The band, dressed in white T-shirts and jeans and looking eerie with white powder on their faces and hair, played familiar music that alternated between heavy disco and soft mood stuff. Tim and I started to dance, and he was great.

As we moved around on the dance floor in perfect union, a lot of couples gave us big hellos, and I began to realize that I was the center of attention.

"Let's sit down for a while with the guys," Tim suggested when the band took a break, and he led me over to his friends who had pulled folding chairs into a sprawling, free-form circle.

"Make way for our leader," joked one unfamiliar boy, and a few kids shuffled around to make a space for us to fill in with chairs of our own.

"Hi, Tim! Hi, Barbara," greeted a lot of familiar faces from the booster club, and I knew they were knocked out by my appearance with Tim.

"Tim, tell us about the fund drive," begged one boy.

"We're here, aren't we," Tim answered jovially. "Business was very, very good."

"But, the work's not over," I whispered to him.

"That's right. Barbara is reminding me that the work is far from over. When the oranges and grapefruit come in next month, we've got to get them out to our customers."

"That means we'll be getting our new intramural T-shirts?" demanded another kid.

"I don't see why not," he responded. I was hoping he'd say more about all the work left to do on the fund drive, but suddenly it was obvious he had lost everyone's attention. Turning to see what was so fascinating, I realized Robin and Bud were standing in the middle of the gym floor.

At first, it was hard to tell who they were. All I saw were tall, slim figures dressed in silver and white, he in a three-piece white suit with a silver bow tie and silver top hat, she in a low-cut white gown glittering with pearly sequins, a sparkling necklace, and a wreath of silver-and-white artificial flowers wrapped around the top of her head.

I drew my breath as did everyone else, including Tim. Suddenly the band, back from its break, struck up with "Dreams, dreams, you're in my dreams," as the couple, Robin and Bud, waltzed slowly around the floor as if they owned the place.

"Aren't they incredible," I heard a voice say in the distance.

"Do I ever love that tune," sighed Tim into my ear, and he started to hum as Robin and Bud continued to monopolize the floor.

Burning with jealousy at Robin's grand entrance, I was furious to hear "Dreams" being played for her. After all, it was my parents' song, a song I was grudgingly coming to see as something that belonged to me and Tim.

When it was finally over, the band switched over to the raucous Rolling Stone tune, "Satisfaction."

"Come on," urged Tim, pulling me out onto the floor. We started to dance, and Tim, who had removed his jacket and loosened his tie, was moving with unbecoming abandon. Mortified, I was sure he was trying to upstage Robin.

But the frenzied moment passed quickly, and soon Tim had settled back into a more laid-back pace. We spend the rest of the evening dancing together and talking to Tim's friends when the band took its breaks. It was mostly sports talk, and at one point, when I found myself trying to understand a discussion about some ruling made by a coach at a recent basketball game, I realized that if I were going to spend more time with Tim, I was going to have to become an expert in North Hollow sports, basketball in particular.

Glancing around the gym, I saw Susan off in another group with Matt, and I almost excused myself to say hello until I remembered that Susan and I had hardly spoken since the day before she had had her tooth pulled. Being on the outs with her for long was no fun at all, and I resolved to patch up our differences as soon as possible.

Meanwhile, I was at the winter dance with Tim Halpern, living out a dream that had been dancing around in my head for nearly half a year. It seemed incredible that so much had happened since that first time I had seen him back in September. I closed my eyes contentedly as we danced close.

In between numbers, I asked Tim if he wanted to dance with anyone else. "I really don't mind," lied the masochist in me.

"Don't be silly, why should I dance with anyone

else? You're just terrific," Tim told me, and I breathed easier. Never much good at sports, I had always enjoyed dancing, and his reassurance was comforting.

Suddenly, it was 1:30 in the morning. The band played its final number, and the dance was over. It had been so much like I had hoped it would be, I wished it would never end.

That Robin had been the undeniable (though self-crowned) queen of the dance bothered me not at all. Tim had chosen me as his date, and he hadn't wanted to dance with anyone else, not even her.

So when Tim drove me home and took me into his arms outside the front door for that long-awaited kiss, all the magic that I had dreamed about for months and months came true.

It was a warm kiss; it was a nice kiss; and being so close to that gorgeous face in the freezing night air felt terrific. Sending my heart racing, it created an instant desire for more.

"A great evening," Tim told me, our frosty breaths mingling.

"I had a great time, too."

"Will you go out with me again?" he asked. "You're so good for me, so down to earth."

"Of course," I answered, not believing what I was hearing.

"It's so nice to spend time with such a pretty, serious girl. You're such a good dancer, too, and a great kisser." This was said without a hint of humor.

But, I could only laugh. "Thanks a lot, and I'll see you in school." I knew I should invite him in for hot chocolate or something, but I really needed to get away to sort out my thoughts. He gave me another sweet kiss, waved, and was gone.

Opening the front door and going upstairs to my room, still wearing my winter coat, I was looking forward to being alone. But as I was getting undressed, Mom suddenly appeared at the door in her elegant silk bathrobe.

"How was it?" she whispered.

"Fine, but Mom, you waited up for me," I complained. "I'm not a baby, you know."

"I know, but this was kind of a big night for us, too. Daddy fell asleep, but he *is* going to want to know all about everything in the morning. Good night, sweetie. Sweet dreams!"

I got into bed determined to review in my mind every dance, every conversation, every moment of the kisses I had shared with Tim. It had been, I thought, an evening of glory. But instead, I fell fast asleep and relived the evening in my dreams.

But it wasn't the kind of savory recreation I would have planned at all. Instead, Tim and I were standing alone in the middle of the gym floor, wearing silver-and-white silk basketball uniforms. Together we ran up and down the gym floor, shooting baskets. The crowd, dressed all in white, cheered their approval, but I never knew whether Tim and I were playing on the same side or against each other.

"Hello princess," boomed Dad as I entered the kitchen the next morning. He was wearing a big, white apron with "Superchef" printed across the chest. "Tell us about your evening."

"What's to tell? I had a great time."

"And?" prompted Dad.

"And nothing. The decorations were great, all white and silver; the band was pretty good; and Tim's a terrific dancer."

"That's it?" he asked, still hoping for more, and I drew my breath in frustration.

"Marty, for Pete's sake," intervened Mom, coming into the room. "Barb's evening is her own business, so let her be." Dad looked at me for some kind of confirmation and then took a deep noisy breath himself.

"I'm sorry, Barbara, your mother's right, of course. It's just that your going out with Timmy Halpern has been such an unexpected thrill for me."

"Enjoy it," Mom told him, "but really, honey, don't push your business and pleasures on Barbara." It was an unusually sensitive speech from Mom and silently I cheered.

10

As I walked up the steps of school that Monday morning, I realized life was going to be a lot different for me at North Hollow High from now on. Kids I barely knew were giving me big, friendly greetings. Even Sandy looked at me strangely that morning, and his lack of communication was driving me crazy. Lately, he barely acknowledged me, and I really missed his friendship.

About fifteen minutes into the study hall period, I got the feeling that Sandy was working on a drawing for me, and I looked forward to receiving it.

It didn't take long, and in a few moments I found myself staring at a sketch of myself holding hands with Tim. Sandy had captured us without question, and it would almost have been a complimentary drawing, too, if Sandy hadn't drawn me hunched over. Pictured on my back were the words North Hollow High and underneath he had written:

"I've heard through the underground that you're our first lady now. I hope you'll remember me when it comes time to make appointments. I'd like to do the official portrait."

"I think you'd be better as Secretary of Offense," I wrote back. "You know, all I did was go to one dance with the guy," I reminded him, hoping to put things in perspective.

"It doesn't take much around here," he wrote back.

"So I've noticed."

Without work to do in the booster office, there was no way or place I could count on seeing Tim, and I went through the day with my eyes darting along hallways and through every crowd I passed. He didn't turn up anywhere, and finally, during eighth period, I wandered over to the gym, where I knew he'd be practicing.

It was a giant, new-looking building, which had been built behind the school; the only reason I ever went there before was to attend required phys ed classes.

As I stepped into the gym lobby, the air changed abruptly from nippy to soggy, and it took a few moments for my nose to adjust to the distinctive gym odor. Out on the court, the boys were running up and down in some official-looking formation, and it wasn't hard to spot Tim in the center. He wore a red sweatband around his forehead and some other sort of band around his elbow. Watching him charge back and forth, I somehow knew that he would never miss a shot.

When the coach blew his whistle and yelled "three-minute break," Tim grabbed a small towel from the bench and came trotting over to see me.

"How ya doing, Barbara," he greeted. "I'm really glad you could drop by."

"There was nothing to do today at the booster office."

"Isn't that a relief!"

"Yeh," I agreed, but actually I was feeling a pang of loss and confusion. Did this mean that from now on I was going to have to seek Tim out at the gym? Yuck. It was a revelation that left me feeling uneasy.

"If you can stick around another forty minutes or so, I'll give you a lift home," he offered.

"That would be fun," I agreed. We talked a little while, and when the whistle blew, Tim raced back into the fray. While watching Tim and the basketball team run up and down the court a few million more times didn't constitute the most inspiring forty minutes I had ever spent, I was right about one thing. Tim never did miss a shot.

When practice was finally over, I walked Tim to the stairs in the lobby, then he went down to the locker room to get cleaned up. Clutching my books, I was staring into the glass cases filled with winged silver trophies when Robin and Laurel emerged together from downstairs.

"Hello, Barbara," said Robin in as sweet a tone as her nasal voice would permit. "I thought you were only into oranges?"

"Variety is the spice of life," I informed her, hoping my snippy rejoinder would show her how her attempt at humiliation had failed. But as we stood there glaring at each other, a crowd of basketball players ran up the stairs, Tim among them. "Hi, girls," he greeted. "Only one more day until the big game. We're counting on you to be great out there with those pom-poms." Then, turning to me he said, "All set, Barbara?" I nodded my head and glided out the door that he held open for me.

When we got into the car, Tim put "Dreams" on the tape deck, and then we took off toward my house. "How'd you like practice?" he asked me.

"It was fun. I've never seen you play before."

"Never?" He was surprised.

"No, and you're so good!"

"Thanks. You know, this game on Wednesday means a lot to me. It's my last shot at the state championships. Pro scouts will be there, and it's never too soon to start making an impression."

"I can't believe you won't be a pro someday."

"I certainly intend to work at it. Meantime, I'll be looking for you at the game Wednesday."

"I'll be there," I promised.

We had pulled up in front of my house. Leaning over, Tim gave me a quick kiss. "Bye, Barbara. You're excellent."

"Bye, Tim, and thanks for the ride." The most gorgeous guy in the world just said he liked me! Slamming the car door, I floated into the house on a fluffy white cloud.

The game against Bellaire turned out to be a real battle. I sat in the bleachers with everyone else in the school, watching the two teams clatter up and down, fighting for control of the ball. Suddenly, Tim grabbed it out of the air and took off down the court toward North Hollow's basket. Tightly guarded by blue-and-white Bellaire players, Tim managed to break away just enough to shoot and make a basket.

The North Hollow fans went wild, I with them, and from the bleachers the cheerleaders started chanting and clapping, "Go team go. Go team go," which everyone echoed and amplified into a frenzy. The score on the big board now read, North Hollow 86, visitors 87, and time was running out.

Suddenly, there was a mad scramble and the sound of a whistle. The referee, dressed in a black-and-white striped shirt, motioned stiffly toward the North Hollow basket. As he held up two fingers, the North Hollow fans went berserk.

"What's happened?" I whispered to a girl next to me, unable to contain my curiosity.

"That blond Bellaire guy fouled Tim!" she gushed, "and now Tim's got two free throws. This could do it for North Hollow. This could bring us over the top!"

As Tim took his stance at the foul line, members of each team lining up on either side, the North Hollow spectators were ominously silent.

Tim took a deep breath while everyone else held tight to the bleachers. Swoosh, the first shot went through the hoop. We all went wild and then settled down quickly for the final all-important shot. Team members along the foul lines were now frozen with anticipation. It was another perfect shot, and North Hollow now led Bellaire by one fragile point!

With fifteen seconds on the clock, the whistle blew for one last desperate time-out. After brief council, the teams came back to fight out the remaining seconds of the game. The scrambling was fierce, but somehow North Hollow managed to prevent Bellaire from getting that fatal shot.

When the dissonant buzzer finally rang, the North Hollow crowd emptied out onto the gym floor to congratulate the team and each other. It was a jubilant mob scene, and I knew it would be a while before I found a clear path to Tim.

I turned to examine the crowd and realized that Sandy Moore was coming toward me. Tipping his hand in greeting, he said not a word.

"Great game," I said to him, wondering if there could be any dispute.

"I'll say this for North Hollow," he agreed, "we do excel in basketball."

"But did you like it?" I persisted.

"What's not to like?" he questioned, before drifting away into the crowd.

I'm not sure how long it took, but after a few intense minutes, the crowd began to thin, and I got closer to the bench where the North Hollow team was clustered. Tim, shaking hands with some of the Bellaire players, was grinning from ear to ear. Then, as if he sensed my presence, Tim turned to me.

"Tim, you were fantastic," I enthused. "Everyone is so excited."

"Thanks, Barbara," he responded, giving my arm a quick, friendly squeeze. "Listen, Barbara, we're having a quicky victory party downstairs. Come on down, if you can, and I'll drop you home later. How about it?"

"Sounds like fun," I told him.

"Great, I'll be cleaned up in ten minutes."

The chaos downstairs was even more intense than

on the gym floor, probably because it was such a confined space. It felt great to be part of the "in" crowd, something I had been dreaming about for months, but all I heard around me was basketball, basketball, basketball. Suddenly, I felt that all-too-familiar urge to get on to other topics.

Driving me home after the victory celebration, Tim was uncharacteristically quiet.

"A penny for your thoughts," I offered, hoping his thoughts had finally shifted from the game.

"Just thinking ahead to Albany and the state championships."

"Oh." I tried to hide my disappointment. "When is it?"

"Week after next, and we're likely to meet much stiffer competition there than the Bellaire team. We've really got to get our act together between now and then." He lapsed into silence again, and this time I didn't bother to intrude.

I felt too wiped out to participate much in the dinner conversation, almost as if I had played basketball with Tim, and afterward I crawled upstairs to do my homework. But concentration was impossible, and I ended up staring at my books as the minutes flipped by on the digital clock. The roar of the gym played over and over in my head, and finally I threw down my books, grabbed my coat, and ran next door to Susan's house.

"Hello stranger," greeted Mrs. Hanover at the front door. "Susan's up in her room."

Afraid she wouldn't talk to me, I knocked softly at Susan's door.

"Susan, it's me, Barbara."

"Oh, hi! Come on in." Her tone was guarded.

"How have you been?" I asked.

"Fine, and you?"

"Okay." There was silence, and I could see she wasn't going to make it easy. "Listen," I told her in a sheepish voice, "I owe you an apology."

"Don't be silly. What for?" She sounded surprised.

"Well, you said something to me as one friend to another, and it made me mad. Now I realize why you said it."

"You mean that stuff about Tim Halpern?" she asked. "You know, Barbara, I'm really sorry about that. I realize now that everybody's taste is different."

"No, I shouldn't have been so sensitive."

"Don't be silly, I really hurt your feelings, and I feel bad. The trouble was, once I said what I did, I didn't know how to undo it. How was the dance?"

"Fine, I really had a good time. And you and Matt?"

"We liked it a lot, too. How are things with Tim?" I could see it took a lot for her to ask, and I appreciated the effort.

Filling her in on the details of the last few weeks, I ended with, "And he's really a sweet guy."

"I never said he wasn't," she pointed out, diplomatically refraining from any elaboration, "and I must confess that I've really been missing you lately; so if I promise to be more understanding, do you think we can be friends again?"

"That's why I came over. I couldn't stand it any longer," I said, starting to sniff.

"Well, it's nothing to cry over," she pointed out.

"I'm just relieved."

"Me too," admitted Susan.

We made plans to walk to school together the next morning, and I went home feeling terrific. As I sat down at my desk to get to the homework I had been avoiding, Dad knocked and came in. "I've been looking all over for you," he told me. "T.J. has decided to drive to Albany in two weeks with Gloria to see the games up there, and he called to ask if we wanted to join him."

"We?"

"You, me, and anyone else who wants to come along. We can watch Timmy play ball, have dinner together, stay in a quaint inn somewhere. It'll be great fun, a real family outing."

"Sure, great," I answered, unable to work up any enthusiasm.

"I knew you'd be excited," he chortled. "I'll just give T.J. a call, and he can get his secretary on it first thing in the morning."

Going back to my homework, I threw myself completely into my French. Tim, basketball, Dad, Mr. Halpern, Albany. There was too much happening too fast, and the only way to deal with it at the moment was to ignore it altogether.

11

You certainly look happy," observed Susan the next morning on the way to school.

"Yeh, it was a great night," I agreed. "You're not going to believe this one. When I got home from your house last night, Dad was waiting for me with a big surprise." I filled her in on the details.

"I'd think you'd be thrilled."

"That is weird, isn't it?" I responded, feeling very glum.

"I hear you and your family are joining us in Albany," Tim greeted me when we met in the hall later that day.

"Yes, your father suggested it, I think."

"Excellent idea," he confirmed, sounding really pleased. "Listen Barbara, we'll be practicing like mad between now and then, so I'll be spending all my spare time at the gym. Drop over whenever you can. We need all the moral support we can get."

"What about student government?" I asked.

"Not much is doing these days, so I think I can safely put everything on hold."

"What about the fruit sale?"

"The shipment isn't due until the week after Albany, so there shouldn't be a problem."

"Whew," I said in mock relief.

"Don't be such a worry wart," he teased, tousling my hair. "Well, see you in the gym."

I spent my afternoons for the rest of the week watching Tim and the rest of the team perfecting their game, and Tim drove me home each evening after practice. I never stopped being thrilled by his incredible good looks. Tense and excited, all his energies focused on the big games in Albany, he never let me forget how he felt about me.

"Barbara, you're an ace to be so loyal about showing up for practice. It can't be much fun for you, but I really appreciate it."

"Nonsense," I denied. "I enjoy watching, and I can see the team getting tighter and tighter every-day. But are you planning to practice all weekend? You'll drop dead before you ever make it to Albany."

"Well, we'll work out for a few hours during the days. How about going to a movie on Saturday night?"

"I thought you'd never ask!"

"It'll have to be an early show," he apologized. "No late-night carousing for me until all this stuff is over."

By the time Saturday night rolled around, I had seen enough basketball to last forever, and I was

looking forward to getting Tim away from the gym
and alone to myself. A movie would give us something new to talk about. I was going to make a
conscious effort to lure him into other topics. But as
we sat downtown in the Art theater on Saturday
night, munching our pop corn and watching the
French Connection with its classic, hair-raising car
chases, I knew there was no way I could turn it into
an intellectual experience. "Whew," was about all
we could manage as we walked over to Merkens for
a quick snack.

It was a freezing night, and Tim silently put his
arm around me to keep me warm. As we walked, my
mind seethed with plans. Once inside Merkens, I
would order a hot chocolate, which I would sip at a
leisurely pace while Tim and I talked about other
movies we had seen.

As it turned out, my hopes were dismally crushed
because the moment we walked into the noisy old-
fashioned ice cream parlor with its red leather
booths and white tiled floor, Tim spied two of his
teammates in the back alcove, working hard on the
electronic games.

"Let's go see what Linley and Smith are up to," he
suggested, leading me back to the big beeping
machines.

So I spent the next hour watching Tim and his
friends trying to beat each others' scores on Pac-Man
until Tim finally glanced at his watch.

"Good grief. It's after ten. We've got to get out of
here!"

Leaving without hot chocolate or any kind of
interesting discussion, we drove home in silence.

"Sorry again, to make it such a quicky," Tim apologized as he stopped the car in front of my house, "but I did warn you."

"Are you sure you don't want to come in for some cookies and hot chocolate?" I invited.

"No, not tonight, thanks." He leaned over and gave me a businesslike kiss. "See you in school," he whispered.

I let myself into the house as Tim drove away and went upstairs before anyone could intercept me. I knew from the lighted windows on the third floor that someone was working up there, but I didn't know if I'd bump into anyone in the living room or den.

What's going on here? I wondered in the privacy of my room. Feeling frustrated and disappointed, I knew something was not right. My head was a mess.

I thought about Tim's soft, sweet kiss, but I also thought about the rest of our time together. Being with the real Tim somehow wasn't as thrilling as seeing Tim the stranger rushing through the hall in school or making stirring announcements from the stage or even out competing on the basketball court.

From upstairs, I could hear the sounds of the piano and harmonic voices trying out snatches of tunes. My parents were at work together. Relieved that they were too engrossed to cross-examine me about my date with Tim, I was also hit with a revelation, and I wasn't so sure I was happy to have it.

Mom and Dad were performers who had fans all over the world. At their concerts, I knew people idolized them, hanging on every note they uttered, every statement they made. It was funny trying to

imagine how these people would feel if they got to
know my folks as real people with real habits. But it
was important to be fair. A lot of people would learn
to love Mom and Dad once they got to know them,
just as a lot of people would be turned off to them.
The point was that when they stood on stage in the
limelight, they were far away and perfect.

The image of the stage held clear in my mind as I
substituted people in the spotlight. Suddenly it was
Tim who was so far away and perfect. Except now I
was beginning to see him as a real person. Tim was a
sweet enough guy, for all his gorgeous looks. The
trouble was, I had the gnawing feeling he wasn't for
me.

What! I was completely horrified. How could I,
Barbara Lane, ever think such a thing? I felt like
crying.

Monday morning was freezing cold. Was I ever
getting sick of winter! As Susan and I meandered up
the sidewalk that bordered the school's circular
driveway, we saw a huge gray tractor trailer truck
parked there, taking up so much space that the
yellow school bus population was barely able to fit
around it. Mr. Broome, the assistant principal, was
standing nearby in his storm coat clutching a clip-
board and having an animated discussion with the
driver of the truck who was leaning back, unimpressed.

"This here fruit's got to go now 'cause my next
load goes to White Plains," the driver was explaining
to Mr. Broome.

"I appreciate that, my man, but according to my
schedule, the fruit isn't due for another two weeks."

Susan and I hovered nearby, listening to the conversation.

"Look guy, most folks would be glad to have this stuff early."

"I suppose so," Mr. Broome conceded. "You might as well start unloading."

"You want the oranges out here on the sidewalk?" asked the driver. "They'll get ruined by the cold."

"No, no, of course not. I'll have to find an empty office for you. Grab a carton and follow me."

"Can't do," objected the driver.

"Why in heaven's name not?"

"Not in my contract."

"What!"

"That's right mister. Like I said, I'd be glad to leave the load here, but in this freeze it'll be wrecked quick as a wink."

Mr. Broome rubbed a hand across his face.

"Susan, I think I've got to do something here," I whispered. "Uh, Mr. Broome, I'm Barbara Lane, and I'm in the booster club. Are these the oranges and grapefruits for our sale?"

"Yes, they are, young lady, and we're having a problem here. We've got to get the fruit inside before it gets frozen and before the whole school is thrown into a traffic turmoil. Where's Halpern?" snapped Mr. Broome. "Isn't he responsible for all this?" Mr. Broome looked at his watch. "It'll take ten minutes to find out what study hall he's in."

"It's 403," I said.

"Fine. I'll go and get him on the intercom. I sure hope he's got his crew lined up for this stuff!" He disappeared up the steps, and while we waited for his return, Susan's boyfriend Matt came down the walk with two other boys.

"Hi, Matt," I called when he was still a few feet away, "I've got a huge favor to ask."

"Watch out for this one," Susan warned them.

Quickly, I described the problem with the oranges and the grapefruit. "Sure Barbara, I don't mind," Matt told me.

"Guys, what do you think?" His friends agreed easily too, and I breathed a sign of relief.

"Halpern's not here yet," panted Mr. Broome as he rushed toward us. "Caught somewhere out there in the traffic, I should imagine." Cars and buses were now parked at a standstill in the driveway and all the way out into the main street. Frantic honking was helping to create genuine chaos.

Our group stood at the back while the driver climbed into the truck and started moving crates forward.

"Where shall we put this stuff, Barbara?" Matt asked, and I turned to Mr. Broome for help.

"Don't you kids have an office downstairs?" he asked.

"Yes, but I don't have a key."

"I've got the master," he said, jingling a chain heavy with keys.

Matt and his two friends and Susan and I started lugging the crates inside on a battered padded platform with wheels that the driver grudgingly lent us, but the more we took from the truck, the more crates there seemed to be.

"You really did some number selling fruit," congratulated Susan, standing next to me.

"Yeh," I agreed. "Tim managed to spark a huge chain reaction in the kids here."

"I wonder where our great leader is now?" she mused.

I did too. When the truck finally pulled away, leaving two offices overflowing with fruit, I knew Tim Halpern, student leader, had a huge job ahead of him.

I missed homeroom altogether that morning, but so did a lot of people, and by the time I limped into study hall, Mr. Broome had made an announcement on the public address system that students caught in the unfortunate driveway traffic jam would be excused for lateness, within reason, thereby destroying any plans Bradshaw might have been hatching to render punishment.

Sandy was at his desk studying his French text when I arrived. I would have liked to have done the same thing, but I was too overwhelmed with thoughts of fruit and Tim.

"Hey, Chiquita, I hear your famous fruit created quite a jam this morning," he scribbled in a note that he slipped on my desk.

"Yes," I wrote back, "about a million oranges and grapefruits arrived more than a week early at exactly the wrong time of day, and then the driver wouldn't bring the stuff inside because he said it wasn't in his contract!"

"That shouldn't have been a problem for our president and his all-star team," he sent back.

"Except they didn't seem to be around. I ended up drafting my friend Susan's unsuspecting boyfriend Matt and some friends of his. And now, there are so many crates of fruit, both the booster office and the room next door are overflowing." My problems seemed to be increasing with every word I wrote.

"Where do you go from here?"

"Who knows! This should rightfully be Tim and Robin's problem, not mine. Mr. Broome was going to fish Tim out of his first-period class."

"Good luck," Sandy wrote back before immersing himself once more in French.

I looked frantically for Tim all day, and by the time eighth period rolled around, I knew I'd have to go to the gym. What I couldn't get out of my mind was the enormous task that Tim, Robin, and the booster club had set up.

It was one thing to see citrus fruit counted on paper and yet another to have to deal with volumes and volumes of the real thing. Tim had thought up this project with the best intentions, but would he follow through to its successful conclusion?

When I got to the gym, Coach Mudd was blowing his whistle to give his panting team a three-minute break. Tim looked up from behind his towel and saw me sitting in the bleachers.

Running over, he greeted me with, "How are you doing, Barbara?" Breathing heavily, he glistened with a fine layer of sweat. "Mr. Broome tells me the fruit arrived this morning and is now safely stored downstairs. Caused quite a mob scene, too, from what I hear," he chuckled. "Oh well, I can't say this is the greatest week for it to have gotten here, but what can we do? It'll just have to sit there till the guys and I get done with Albany."

"Are you serious? It can't sit there for a week!"

"I don't see why not. It does in the supermarket."

"But it's refrigerated there!"

"Oh Barbara, you're such a worrywart. A week isn't going to make a difference."

"Listen, Tim, you guys may be too busy with basketball to care, but somehow those oranges and grapefruit have got to get out of here before it's too late."

"It's your job, if you want it," he offered generously, "but I have to say that if you insist on doing it this week, you're on your own as far as the basketball team is concerned."

"What's wrong with the rest of the school?"

"Nothing. You've just got to motivate them, that's all."

"I can't believe this is Tim Halpern, school president, talking!"

"Barbara, believe me, I don't intend to shirk my responsibilities. But first things first!"

Mr. Mudd blew the whistle, signaling the end of time-out. "I'll talk to you later," Tim said. Giving me a pat on the head, he rushed back on the court.

"Hey, I need a key to the booster office," I yelled after him.

"Robin's got one downstairs," he yelled back.

Downstairs, the cheerleaders were standing around in their gym suits watching Laurel demonstrate a neat turn and jump. "Excuse me," I interrupted without any feelings of discomfort that I might usually have felt, "I need to speak to Robin for a moment about something important."

"Sure," said Laurel, "go ahead."

Robin came forward, a funny look in her eye.

"Could you come in the hall a moment?" I requested, knowing desperately that I didn't want to confront her in front of everyone else. She followed grudgingly and, once outside, she turned on me before I could say another word.

"I suppose you came about those stupid crates," she accused.

"Yes."

"Well, Tim said we could forget about them until after Albany."

"Great," I assured her, "by then they may be half-rotten. Listen, Robin, I just spoke to Tim and told him I was going to get the distribution under way. I didn't think it could wait."

"Well rooty-toot for you," she jeered. "You can count me out for this week. Next week is soon enough."

"Fine. There are plenty of other kids around here who can help. Just give me the key to the office."

"What!"

"You heard me. Just give me the key."

"Oh, very well." I followed her back into the practice room, where she dug the key out of her bag and practically threw it at me.

Without a word, I took it and headed back to the main building. Climbing the stairs down to the basement office, I wondered if I was being a fool. What if Tim were right? But then again, what if he were wrong? The disaster would be unfathomable.

I unlocked the door and squeezed my way through the crates to the big desk, which had miraculously been left bare. The aroma of oranges and grapefruit was overpowering but delicious. Though there was barely room for me to pull out the big chair, somehow I managed to squirm in behind the huge desk.

I sat down feeling very lost indeed.

"This is what I call a Florida Room," said a strong male voice from the doorway, interrupting my blank thoughts. It was Sandy. "I figured you might need help," he continued, while inching his way around the crates, "but never did I expect this."

"If you think this is bad," I told him, my voice quavering slightly, "you should see the other room. There's even more in there! On second thought, forget it. I have to do something about getting a key."

"Where's Halpern and the rest of the troops?" Sandy wanted to know.

"Down at the gym, practicing for the big Albany competition." I filled him in on my aggravating conversations with Tim and Robin.

"So now what?" he asked, when I was done.

"I haven't the faintest idea."

"Well, take a deep breath, and let's analyze this situation. If this stuff had arrived at the right time, then what would have happened?" he asked.

"Tim would have announced its arrival at assembly, and everybody would have picked up their orders, except now Tim and probably the whole basketball contingent won't get around to it until after next weekend. Don't you think it might rot if it sits here that long?"

"Well, it's not going to improve with age, that's for sure. Maybe you can rustle up some new recruits to cover for the otherwise engaged basketball team. Will Halpern at least announce that the fruit's here during tomorrow's assembly? There's a whole school of sports maniacs out there."

"Yes, I suppose so," I conceded without much hope.

"You have one other choice, of course."

"What's that?"

"You can dump the whole deal on Halpern and walk away. This really is his brainstorm after all, and he deserves any headaches he gets." Sandy looked at me hard, and I stared right back.

"No," I answered. "I said I'd do it, and I meant it, even if it kills me!" I said hotly.

"Well, if that's how you feel, at least let me know what I can do to help."

"Sandy, are you really sure you want to get involved? You've never made any secret of your feelings about this fruit sale thing." I was remembering some of Sandy's prophetic drawings and what his mother had told me about him.

"I may have made some nasty comments," he conceded, "but I never said I wouldn't help out in a pinch. Just consider it my contribution toward the basketball team's new gold-plated sneakers." We both laughed.

I just couldn't bring myself to meet Tim down at the gym for my usual ride home. The anger inside of me burned slow but steady. Instead, I walked home with Sandy, each of us carrying whatever oranges we could manage in addition to our books.

"You know, this is another problem we're going to have to work out," I told Sandy as we walked along, "How am I going to deliver my orders? I think I sold at least a gross of oranges."

"I think I have an idea about something we can give everyone when they pick up their order," he told me. "But I'll have to tell you later, when I'm sure."

We were at the turnoff to my street. I hesitated a moment, wanting to say something, but Sandy hardly gave me a chance.

"So Barbara," he told me abruptly, "talk to you later," and with that, pockets bulging, he headed down the street.

Turning down Cheshire, I had a funny feeling. Despite all this craziness, one nice thing had happened. After all these months, Sandy Moore had managed to look me straight in the eye!

I found Gram in the kitchen when I got home, and I delivered the oranges to her. "Lovely," she said, eyeing the round orange balls. "Let's have a taste and see how they are." Cutting one into convenient eighths on a small Lucite board, we each had a juicy mouthful. "Mmm, fantastic," we agreed simultaneously.

"Gram, are these the best oranges you've ever tasted!" I asked with pride.

"Pretty much," she conceded, "but where is the rest of my order?"

"Still at school. I'll bring them home tomorrow if I can."

"Darling, just how much fruit are you responsible for?"

I laughed. "About a million pounds, I think. You're not going to believe what I'm about to let myself in for." I told her about Tim, basketball, and the oranges. "Did I do the wrong thing? Do *you* think the fruit can sit there for a week or two?"

"No, not if it's going to still taste like this."

"Do you think I'm nuts to try to take this thing over?"

"Nuts? Yes. But that's not to say I wouldn't have done the same thing in your place. You know, somehow I would have expected more from that young fellow, but I'm glad to see there are some young people around here who are growing up with a sense of responsibility."

"Thanks, Gram."

"Now Barbara, from all you've said, I can see you may need assistance. If you need me with the car, just give me enough notice and I'll make myself available."

"Thanks Gram. I really appreciate the offer, but I hope it won't come to that. But Gram, could you not mention this stuff to Mom and Dad? I don't think I could stand to discuss it with them right now."

"No, I can appreciate that." She gave me an affectionate, understanding hug, and I went upstairs to start my homework.

After dinner when I called Tim, he greeted me as if he hadn't a care in the world.

"Tim, I've got some serious fruit sale business to discuss with you."

"Shoot."

"Well, I've decided to start the distribution immediately, tomorrow, even if you guys are too busy to help."

"Ambitious girl."

"It's more conscience than ambition. Tomorrow is weekly assembly, and I need you to announce that the fruit is here and that kids should come down to pick up their orders." In hope of drumming up some new recruits, I filled him in rather elaborately on what else I wanted him to tell the student body.

"Whew. Would you rather make the announcement yourself?" he offered.

I thought for a moment. "Well, the truth is, I think it has more clout coming from you."

"Barbara, how can I remember it all?"

"It's not that much," I assured him. "Look, I'll say it one more time, and you can take notes."

"Fine." I went over my idea again, slowly.

"I missed you after practice today," Tim told me when I was done.

"I had a pressing date with oranges and grapefruit," I told him.

As soon as we hung up, the phone rang again. It was Sandy. "I've got the greatest shopping bags for fruit," he announced. "Some new wonder plastic that's supposed to hold up to a hundred pounds. Each bag should be good for a couple of dozen oranges at least. Of course, they do say *North Hollow Herald* on the side."

"They sound perfect."

"My father's going to drop them off at school tomorrow."

"Great. Listen, Sandy, I spoke to Tim about making the announcement at assembly tomorrow afternoon. Can you help out at the office afterward when people come down for their fruit?"

"Sure, and I'll see if my friend Judson can come along."

"And I'll see if Susan and Matt will pitch in."

"Now all we need are kids to show up and take away the fruit."

"There's no reason why Tim can't continue to spark the same enthusiasm he's always gotten."

"Yeh," said Sandy in a markedly dull voice, abruptly ending our conversation.

I went back to my homework, but not before I spent a few minutes thinking about Tim's remarkable leadership abilities. In light of my task ahead, I was praying they would be as strong as ever, especially since I knew that the flame of excitement he had kindled in me was in danger of flickering.

12

"Do you think you can find it in your heart to help out with the fruit sale?" I asked Susan the next day.

"I don't know, why? What's Tim ever done for me?"

"Tim aside, would you do it for me?"

"For you Barbara? Of course, no question."

"Whew," I joked, "because I'm going to need your help for a while today right after assembly. Do you think Matt might help out, too?"

"Probably, the whole citrus scene has him in stitches. He's been busy computing how many gallons of orange juice he could squeeze and stuff like that."

"Oh, how many gallons?" I was suddenly interested.

"He doesn't have an answer yet. Maybe by this afternoon he'll know."

I held a meeting of my new booster club staff during lunch, and we sat around hashing out a foolproof distribution system. Between classes, I ordered a key from Mr. Broome for the other storeroom.

Tim made an appropriately rousing announcement at assembly, and I was delighted when a mob of students turned up at the booster office to pick up orders. Sandy, his friend Judson, Susan, Matt, and I set to work, and by the end of an hour and a half we had managed to get rid of at least thirty-five cases of fruit. Our system really worked!

"I'd really love to clear the offices before the weekend," I told my cohorts when the first day's crowd had cleared.

"Good luck," said Susan with a sigh. "What we really need is a station wagon," suggested Sandy.

"Has anyone here even got a license?" Matt asked, and we all groaned in frustration.

"Oh, wait a minute," I announced. "My grandmother offered to help yesterday, and she has a station wagon." The three boys looked at me with disbelief.

"You guys won't believe Barbara's grandmother." Susan laughed. "She is one nifty person."

"Well, we're ready and willing to lug the fruit if she can drive us around town," promised Matt.

"I'll see what I can arrange."

We agreed to meet at lunch again the next day, and I locked the offices, feeling very good about what we had accomplished.

As a group, we started to walk down the hall. But Susan ambled a few doors down to study the bulletin board. I couldn't imagine why.

"Will you look at that," she said, pointing at the board. "There's a note here for Bonnie Street." All of a sudden I was paralyzed, but Susan continued with admirable abandon. "Gee, she lives right near me. I think I'll drop it by on the way home."

"Who is she?" asked Matt.

"Oh, a new girl in town," she told him, slipping the envelope into her bag.

Sandy studied Susan speculatively while I trembled inside. Trying hard to remain calm, I was only thankful that the newspaper office door was closed and that no one else had heard this little dialogue.

Once outside, Judson and Matt took off toward their homes while Susan, Sandy, and I walked together toward our neighborhood.

"You can let me see that note now," I told Susan.

"Why are you making such a big secret of this, Bonnie?" Sandy chuckled.

"Well, it really is kind of sticky for me," I told him with annoyance.

"Calm down, Barbara," suggested Susan. "Why don't you take a look at what the note says before you let this thing get out of control." Taking it from her, I put my books and oranges on the ground.

"You guys don't understand at all," I complained, as I read them the brief note. "The editor, Lynn Gardner, wants Bonnie Street to approve some suggested changes in her story before it can be published. Now what am I going to do?" The pleasure of getting rid of thirty-five cases of oranges and grapefruits was completely overshadowed by this latest development, and I knew for sure that my day, if not my week, month, and possibly year, was unalterably ruined.

"The fact is, one way or the other, you're going to

have to own up to the truth if you want to get any further with the paper," said Sandy.

"Rats," I snarled, knowing he was right. "Just what I needed right now."

At home, Gram agreed readily to help out with the car the following afternoon at three thirty and any other time we needed her. At least that was one load off my mind.

Right after dinner I delivered fruit to the nearest neighbors, storing the remainder in our basement refrigerator. Tim called around nine thirty, as I was trying desperately to get to work on my latest history assignment. After asking lightly about the fruit sale, he launched into a ten-minute monologue on his day of practice. But I just wasn't in the mood. Instead, I held the phone to my ear and let his soothing voice provide background music while I thought again about my own problems.

By the time I left for school the next morning, I had grudgingly admitted to myself that Sandy had been right about my pen name. I was going to have to confess, and soon.

"You're letting this fruit sale get the best of you," observed Gram the next morning, as we made our plans to meet at school later in the day.

"It's not that at all," I assured her. "My friends in school have been terrific, and now, with your help, everything seems under control. It's something very different."

"Anything I can do?"

"Not a thing." I sighed.

That afternoon, Susan and Matt went out with Gram in the station wagon to deliver fruit, leaving

Sandy, Judson, and me behind to staff the booster office. After a sudden influx of kids retrieving their orders, the office became very quiet, and I saw the chance to make my dreaded move. Leaving Sandy and Judson to hold down the fort, I slipped down the hall to meet my fate.

Inside the newspaper office, it didn't look all that different from the booster office except that it was twice the size, a wall having been removed between two rooms. And, of course, there were no crates of fruit. It was packed with desks and chairs, and on the walls were bulletin boards plastered with paste-ups of the paper.

My eyes darting uneasily around the room, I saw three or four students, working at desks, with no sign of Mr. Rush.

I took a deep breath as the girl closest to me looked up.

"Is Lynn Gardner here?" I asked.

"Over there," she said, indicating a girl working in a far corner, in what was the equivalent of the other office.

I walked over slowly, wondering how far voices would carry in this vast space. "Lynn?" I asked, my voice full of hesitation, and a pretty girl with wavy ash-blond hair and glasses looked up.

"Uh, I'm Bonnie Street," I continued in a near whisper.

"No kidding! Sit down. We loved your story." I smiled nervously and pulled up a chair as she rummaged through a folder and pulled out my manuscript. "The thing is, both Josh and I feel that it needs a little extra punch to start, which you could easily get by moving the dialogue from the second

paragraph, here, up to the opening of the story."
She pointed to a question mark made in the margin
with blue pencil.

"That seems fine," I agreed. "Are there any other
suggestions?"

"Not that I know of. We're making it our lead
piece in the spring issue. Even our faculty advisor
was enthusiastic, and he's a real stickler."

"Oh, Mr. Rush?"

"Yes, do you know him? He couldn't remember
having had you in class."

"Uh, well that is a little problem." My head was
swimming with confusion, and I had lowered my
voice to a whisper. There was a silence as I sum-
moned up the nerve to confess. "Bonnie Street's not
my real name," I finally admitted with pain. "I'm in
one of Rush's classes, and he hates me desperately.
If he knew who wrote that piece, he'd probably kill it
in a second."

"So we just won't tell him," she offered. "It's
nothing to worry about, I promise."

"There's a little more," I continued, heartened by
her attitude. "You see, the thing is, I'm dying
to work on the paper . . . and, well, with Rush
as the advisor, there's no way it's going to happen."

Lynn was shaking her head, a disgusted look on
her face. "Yes, I know Rush can be weird. He's not
very popular around here." So she understood! But
was there any solution to my problem? I wondered.
"I have some very interesting news for you," she
continued, lowering her voice to a whisper that
matched my own. "Not that many people know this
yet, but Rush won't be around next year."

"What!" I mouthed, my eyes popping out of my head.

Her eyes shifted back and forth across the room, much like mine had, to see if anyone else in the room had caught wind of our conversation. Her eyes sparkled, and her face was covered with a conspiratorial little smirk. "I'm not sure what your problems with him are, but he has a bad reputation for singling out kids and dumping on them with very little provocation."

"You've got it exactly," I confirmed, feeling a rush of warmth toward Lynn.

"Well, he's dumped on his last kid," she whispered.

"What happened?"

"Do you know who Adam Sinclair is? He's a freshman."

"No."

"Obviously neither did Rush when he started to make Adam's life miserable. He's the superintendant's stepson."

"No kidding. How do you know?"

"He's a friend of my brother's."

"So what happened?" I urged.

"It's a long story, but the upshot is that Rush won't be coming back next year to North Hollow High."

"That's the greatest news I've heard all year," I whispered.

"I know," she agreed. "And so Bonnie," she continued in a more reasonable, but still subdued voice, "there's no reason why I can't recommend you for the paper next fall."

"Lynn, that would be fantastic. Will you still be here?"

"Yes, I'm a junior, and next year I'll be editor-in-chief."

"Oh, I can hardly wait," I told her.

"It is fun," she conceded. "Meantime, I hope you're going to keep writing."

"Oh yes, I write in my journal nearly every day, and I'm working on an idea for another story."

"That's terrific. Say," she whispered suddenly, "what's your real name, anyway?"

"Barbara Lane."

I left that office feeling happier than I had felt in a long time and went back down the hall to the booster office. I could hardly wait to share my news with Sandy and Susan. But when I walked in, I was totally surprised to find Tim sitting at the main desk and Sandy off in a corner drawing a picture in his sketchbook of Judson. Somehow, it was completely unnerving to see sparkling, dashing Tim in the same room with introverted, grubby Sandy.

"Tim, what are you doing here?" I asked.

"Coach said we'd been working too hard so he gave us the afternoon off, so get your stuff and I'll drive you home."

"But I have fruit business to take care of."

"It's pretty slow right now. These guys can do it."

"No, I'm not deserting Sandy and Judson," I objected.

"Barbara, it's tapered off," offered Sandy. "We were thinking of calling it a day now anyway."

"Well, what about your oranges and grapefruits?" I demanded of Tim.

"What about them?"

"Aren't you going to take them? What better time than now, when we can give you a hand getting the crates to your car."

"Only if I can drive you home," he persisted.

"Deal," I capitulated.

I looked up his orders in the ledger, and Sandy and Judson packed eight bags of oranges and grapefruits for him. Then we all walked with the shopping bags to the parking lot.

"Thanks, you guys," I told Sandy and Judson once we got the fruit stowed in Tim's back seat and trunk. "See you tomorrow."

Sandy and Judson waved, but Tim didn't say a word until he had started the engine and pulled out of the parking space.

"Where'd you find those two losers?" he demanded.

"Tim, what a thing to say about friends of mine!"

"Well, they look like a pair of turkeys, if you ask me."

"If you mean they're not sports freaks, you're right about that. They're into other things."

"Like what?" he asked, but I didn't think he was really interested.

"I don't have to defend them to you. They're my friends, and they came through on this dumb fruit sale when you and all your buddies around here were too busy. You ought to be thanking them for getting you out of a tight spot, not bad-mouthing them." I was furious, and Tim knew it.

"Okay, okay," he conciliated, "I guess you're right, but they're hardly your style."

"Yeh, I guess," I responded, my thoughts latching

on to his odd comment. My style? Whatever was my
style anyway? For such a long time I had thought
Tim was my style. Now I was thinking it had all been
a big mistake.

On the way home, Tim invited me to the movies
again for Saturday night, the last "quicky," he said,
before Albany. "Things will be a lot better after
that," he promised. "We'll be able to spend a lot
more time together." He gave me a brief kiss, and I
went into the house wondering whether he was right.
Maybe it was our lack of time that was messing
things up.

But Dad was waiting for me in the den when I got
in, wanting to go over, for the hundredth time, the
details of the trip he and T.J. were planning to
Albany. "Mom may even tag along," he told me,
"so we'll plan to do some sight-seeing too. Maybe
hop over to Cooperstown for the Baseball Hall of
Fame."

"Great, Dad," I told him without much enthusiasm, and I escaped upstairs. Looking out my bed-
room window, I saw that Gram's car was missing
from the driveway, and I realized she was still out
with Susan and Matt delivering fruit. I had a rush of
guilt knowing that I wasn't out there with them, but
then I remembered the wonderful interview I had
had in the newspaper office. I was dying to tell
someone the good news.

Susan wasn't home yet, and though she might be
at any moment, I decided to get gutsy and call
Sandy. Why shouldn't I do it again, especially now
that I was starting to feel he was a real friend?

"I wanted to tell you what happened at the
newspaper office this afternoon," I said when Sandy

answered the phone. I described my conversation with Lynn, including the information about Rush's fatal blunder.

"That's terrific news. You must feel pretty darn good," Sandy observed.

"I do, I do," I agreed. "Rush is finally getting what he deserves, I'm getting a break at the paper, and the fruit distribution is going better than I had ever imagined; you'd think I wouldn't have a care in the world!"

"You're not kidding," he joked. "Well, Ms. Success, it's been nice talking to you." Our conversation ended quickly, more quickly than I liked to admit, and I was left to ponder my happiness.

13

Tim was taking me out to the movies again, and though I had dressed carefully, done my hair and makeup, as the clock neared 7:15, I got more and more depressed. I should have been ecstatic, I knew, but instead I felt weird. It was a strange feeling of uneasiness because I couldn't figure out where it was coming from. "Get your act together," I warned myself.

The movie was a cowboy-shoot-'em-up, which I enjoyed although it was hardly the provocative sort of subject I would have chosen. Afterward, we headed to Merkens again, and I began to dread a horrid replay of the previous Saturday night.

But there was no sign of Smith or Linley back in the game alcove, and I breathed a sigh of relief as Tim headed to a private red booth. We both ordered hot chocolate, and while we waited for it to arrive, Tim filled the time with basketball news.

"Tony Miller pulled a muscle in his arm at practice this morning."

"You look worried," I observed.

"I am. You know how much that game means to me."

"Did you deliver any of your fruit to satisfied customers this morning?" I asked, changing the subject.

"Are you kidding? I had to be at practice at ten o'clock."

"So where is all the stuff? You had nearly eight bags, as I remember."

"You don't want to know," he said.

The waitress arrived with our steaming cups of chocolate, mountains of whipped cream on top. Tim began to stir the cream into his drink.

"You know Tim," I started, "as far as I'm concerned, you really blew this whole fruit business."

"What do you mean? We made more money than we ever dreamed of."

"Who do you mean by 'we'?"

"You and me."

"And who else?" I prompted. "What about Susan, Matt, Sandy, Judson, and all the other kids at school who chipped in their time? Don't they count?" I persisted.

"Of course, but it was my idea, and people will still remember it as my fund drive."

"Tim, you were ready to dump the whole thing!"

"No I wasn't. I was just putting it off for a week or two."

"Have you any idea how hard people worked so your precious fund drive would be a success?" I was

yelling, I knew, but it hardly made a dent in the din
of dishes and Saturday night chatter all around us.

"You worked hard, I know that," he assured me.

"Tim, you're missing the point completely. It
wasn't just me. It was me and everyone else. We all
lugged oranges and grapefruits around so you could
have glory! I thought you knew about teamwork."

"Bah," he waved his hand, "as far as I'm concerned, life is just a game of one-on-one."

I might have been a newcomer to basketball, but
his meaning came through loud and clear. I threw
him my dirtiest look, but it flew right by him.

I didn't feel much like talking after that. I was too
furious. But Tim seemed completely unaffected by
my anger, so I just sat back and let him fill the time
with the life story of Coach Mudd. Cool as the
chocolate in his cup, he seemed to think I would
want to hear all about his greatest hero.

I listened patiently, too, watching the expression
on his perfect face. It was horrible to admit, but
true—whatever Tim's personality, he was still nice
to look at.

As he went on and on, I began to have a very
uncomfortable question for myself: Why wasn't Tim
Halpern coming through as the boy of my dreams?

There, I had said it. Tim Halpern was sitting
across the table from me describing how Coach
Mudd was supervising the basketball training of his
five-year-old son, and I was wondering what happened to my own great hero. It wasn't anything I
could answer easily, that's for sure, and the torture
of searching my mind left me speechless.

Tim drove me home well before ten o'clock, and

when we pulled up in front of my house, I jumped out of the car before he could touch me. Something was definitely wrong if I, Barbara Lane, was avoiding a kiss from Tim Halpern.

I was relieved to see Mom and Dad's car still missing from the driveway, and as Tim drove away with a cheerful wave, I unlocked the front door. Jonathan was in the den watching television, a big yellow cat curled up beside him, so I slipped upstairs without saying a word.

But once in my room, I wanted desperately to talk to someone. There was something on my mind, something very heavy, and it needed some air. Susan was out with Matt, I knew, so there was no sense calling her.

Without even taking off my jacket, I walked down the hall to Gram's room and knocked softly on the door. Not that it was closed; I just didn't want to barge in.

"Barbara, how was your evening?" she asked from her chaise, where she sat reading a heavy book.

"Okay, I guess."

"That's nice. She was peering at me over the top of her half-frame reading glasses.

Sitting down on Gram's bed, I began to sniff uncontrollably. "Is it young Halpern?" she asked.

"Uh-huh." I shook my head.

"How so?"

"Well, I haven't told this to anyone, but I've been thinking Tim was the most perfect guy in the world. I even went out of my way to dress differently and be indispensable at the booster office so he'd notice me! When he started asking me out, I was so excited I thought I'd burst. Then Susan had said Tim was a creep, and I got really mad."

"That wasn't very nice of her was it?"

"No, but she really didn't mean anything bad by it. Now I can see what she was talking about. Tim is really just for Tim! Oh Gram, I'm so miserable!" I started to sniff again.

"You know," Gram said gently, "some people are like that."

"But Gram, I'm so disappointed!" I wailed.

"No, it's more than that," she told me after I sniffed a few more times. "I think you're really furious."

I laughed through my tears. "Yeh, you're right. I *am* furious, and I feel cheated, too."

"But, why not look at it another way?" she suggested. "You set out to do something, and you succeeded. That's something, don't you think?"

"Yes," I agreed, and suddenly I wasn't crying anymore. Gram handed me a tissue, and I dried my eyes. "You know, that's just part of what's been going on." I told her about Mr. Rush and Mom and Dad, my short story, Sandy, and the school newspaper. She shook her head sadly as I described all the painful nuances. "But it's okay now," I concluded. "I set out to get myself a chance to work on the school paper, and I did it!"

"My goodness, you've been busy. This has been some year for you, hasn't it. You should be very proud."

"I am, come to think of it." I gave her a kiss on her soft wrinkled cheek. "Gram, I think something important has just happened. I feel terrific."

Later that night, as I lay in bed I heard Mom and Dad come in the front door humming "Dreams." It was nice to hear them singing together just for fun, even if their dreams and mine weren't exactly the same.

But the next morning at the breakfast table, I realized there was something I was going to have to straighten out.

"Dad, I need to talk to you after breakfast," I whispered.

"I'm rushing out to the club this morning, but if it's short, we can talk in the den before I leave." Gram was watching this little interchange with Dad, so when I nibbled halfheartedly at my breakfast, she had the good grace not to say a word.

Dad took a last sip of coffee and pushed himself away from the table.

Jumping up and running inside before I lost my nerve, I waited while he put on his coat and scarf.

"Now what's so important?" he wanted to know as he adjusted his collar in the mirror.

"It's about next weekend," I started bravely. "I'm not coming."

"What?"

"I'm not coming to Albany with you guys. As it turns out, I'm really not into basketball, Dad, and I'm not planning to see much of Tim once the fruit sale business is cleared away."

"Barbara, what are you talking about?"

"Dad, I know you're in a hurry, so I won't explain every little detail now; but I want you to know how I felt so you can get used to it, and I hope you'll still go without me."

"Barbara, are you sure you know what you're saying. Did you have a fight with Timmy or something?"

"No nothing like that," I assured him. "I'm just not ready for this whole thing."

"Okay, okay." He was looking at his watch. "We'll talk more about it later."

"Fine," I agreed, "But the point is, I'm not going with you to Albany." He gave me a hurried kiss on the cheek, shook his head, and fled out the door.

I went over to Susan's house as soon as I thought everyone would be awake to tell her about my revelation.

"You were right the whole time about Tim," I said, "and I owe you an apology." She was still wearing her nightgown, bathrobe, and slippers.

"What happened?" Her face lit up with a mischievous grin.

"Nothing really, except that the more I see him, the more I realize where he's at."

"Where's that?"

"Out there on the big basketball-court-in-the-sky."

"Did you tell him how you feel?" she asked.

"I tried, but talk about dense! Everything goes right past him."

"So what are you going to do?"

"Who knows, but I'm not worried. He used to say how much he liked me, but you know, I don't think it'll hurt him one bit when I tell him I don't want to see him anymore. I did tell my father this morning that I wasn't going to Albany next week."

"No kidding. You're really serious!"

"Absolutely," I confirmed. "Now talk about a person with a broken heart. Do you think he'll recover?"

We had a good laugh together, and when it was over I continued in a more sober direction. "But you know, Susan, guys are really weird."

"You mean people are weird," she corrected.

"I guess, but I'm thinking about Tim and Sandy."

"How so?"

"Well, Tim, from the way he looks and acts on the outside, seems like the greatest guy in the world. Sandy, on the other hand, the original introvert, came through when I needed help and turned out to be everything nice that I expected from Tim. Too bad he's not talking to me."

"What?"

"Yeh, I called him the other day to tell him my big news, and he practically hung up on me."

"What big news?"

"Oh Susan, I forgot to tell you about the newspaper. It's so exciting!" I told her about what happened with Lynn Gardner, Mr. Rush, and me.

"Congratulations," she beamed. "This has been some week for you!" She gave me a big uncharacteristic hug. "Now listen," she told me abruptly, "I have something important to do now, so would you mind leaving?"

"I don't get it," I told myself as I walked home. "Susan's the weirdest of the bunch."

I went home and got to work on my journal. Filling page after page, I had a lot to say. Then the phone rang, and Gram called up the stairs to say it was for me. This may be the moment to confront

Tim, I thought to myself as I picked up the phone.
But instead, it was Sandy Moore.

"Hi, what are you doing?" he asked.

"Writing in my journal."

"Would you like to meet me when you're done,
and we'll go for a walk. I'd really like to talk to you."

"Oh sure," I agreed, wondering what he was up
to.

"How much longer do you need to work?"

"Another hour or two," I answered.

"Want to meet me outside at 3:30? We can walk
over to the new portrait show at the museum, unless
you've seen it."

"No, I haven't. That sounds nice."

I worked almost nonstop until 3:15, and suddenly
I was out of words. Washing my face and brushing
my hair, I looked forward to my walk with Sandy.

"Hi," he greeted when I met him outside. "How's
your journal?"

"Fine, thanks. As it turned out, I wrote all
afternoon, until just a few minutes ago."

"Did you need more time?"

"No, I was ready to stop; if nothing else, my arm
was about to fall off."

"By the way," Sandy said, his voice faltering,
"I'm not sure if I told you the other night when you
called how impressed I am about all this newspaper
stuff, and I really am looking forward to reading
your story."

"Thanks a lot. If you're serious, I'll bring a copy
to school."

"Great," he answered, and I think he really meant
it. Looking hard at Sandy, I kept thinking he looked
different, in a nice sort of way.

"You had a haircut," I blurted out before I could stop myself.

"Yeh." He looked down, embarrassed. "I thought it would be nice to see for a change, so I went down to Oscar the barber yesterday. He even gave me a lollipop for being so brave."

"It's nice to *see* you," I complimented.

We started walking downtown to the little Carnegie Museum.

"You did say you haven't been to the new show, right?" he asked.

"Right," I reconfirmed, "if this is the one that just opened."

"But you keep up with the exhibits?"

"I try to, not that I know much about art. Except, I do know what I like. I loved that "Box Art" show they had a few months back, especially the Joseph Cornell boxes with all the birds and balls."

"Yes, they are magical," he agreed. "He had a one-man show last year at the Museum of Modern Art."

"Whose work is in this exhibit?" I asked. "Do you know anything about it?"

"Well," he started slowly, as if marshaling his thoughts. "It's an exhibit of portraits of all types: painting, drawing, sculpture, assemblage. Again, some are by well-known people, some up-and-coming people, and some completely unknown."

"I wonder if there are any portraits of Chiquita Banana," I joked.

"What made you say that?"

"I don't know. It just popped into my head."

"I think you will be surprised," he promised.

"You've seen the exhibit, then?"

"Well, yes, there was an opening party last night."

We walked up the stone steps into the miniature castle. I stopped to pay my admission, but the woman at the front desk said hi to Sandy and waved us on in.

The first gallery was filled with portraits in all dimensions, as Sandy had intimated. They ranged from historic, dusty-looking families sitting primly in their chairs, to contemporary drawings that seemed more like doodles, to incredibly real-looking sculptured wax figures that stood, fully dressed in real clothes and looking as if they were running, in the middle of the room.

Sandy and I walked together slowly through the first room and into the second. As we looked at portrait after portrait, discussing what we saw, I suddenly noticed a frame filled with a series of pencil portraits done in a familiar style.

"Sandy, these are yours!" I said, delighted at my discovery. "They're beautiful."

"Thanks," he said looking down, embarrassed again. I studied the beautifully rendered drawings carefully.

"Sandy, they're of me," I shrieked in a loud whisper.

"Yes, do you mind?"

"No, not really. Besides, you really made me look good," I joked. The portraits, four in all, were of me from the side as I worked or read at my desk in study hall. For the most part, my hand was obscuring my face. But it wasn't the recognizability of my face that made the drawings so nice. It was the beautiful way he had made his lines and shadows and the way he had captured the feeling of my intense concentration.

We looked at the other portraits in the exhibit and then went outside into the fading afternoon.

"Talk about impressed," I told him, as we walked along the sidewalk in town with no particular destination. "Your drawings look wonderful hanging in there, like they really belong. How'd it happen? How'd you get your stuff into the show?"

"A series of coincidences," he explained. "From going to all the exhibits, I've gotten to know the people who work there. Somehow I mentioned to Peter Sanborne, the director, that I liked to draw. I showed him a sketchbook, and he wanted to see more and more and more. Let me tell you, there was a lot to look at, too! He singled out those drawings of you as my best series and asked if he could put them in this show."

"Why didn't you ever tell me? It's so exciting!"

"I don't know. For one thing, I guess I didn't really believe it was going to happen. For another thing, I was a little afraid of you."

"Of me? I can't believe it."

Sandy was silent for a moment. "You know, Barbara, I feel as though we've been friends for a long time."

"I feel that way, too," I said, beaming.

"Yet," he continued, as if in pain, "for a long time I could barely work up the nerve to talk to you, to look you in the eye."

"Sandy, I did notice," I told him with a smile, "not that we ever had much trouble communicating."

"But Barbara," he continued, still deadly serious, "the reason I wrote so many notes to you is simple. I was too nervous to talk to you."

"Oh?"

"Well, I wanted to be more to you than just a friend."

"Oh."

"Well, yes, but how in the world could I ever hope to keep up with a school president and a basketball star?"

"Tim?"

"Yes."

I started to laugh and then stopped when I realized he might misunderstand. "Sandy, I have the most embarrassing confession to make. I guess I'm completely transparent, but yes, I did have this incredible crush on Tim for ages. But you know what? The more I got to know him, the more I knew I didn't want to know him. Now I realize that a lot of the stuff you and Susan said about him was true."

"Yes, I know. She told me."

"What!" Suddenly I was furious. "Susan told you?"

"She didn't mean any harm," Sandy defended. "Susan, Matt, and I have become good friends since this fruit sale thing, so Susan called me this morning to say you thought I was mad at you. She said she owed you one, whatever that means. I wanted to tell you I'm really not mad at all. I've been acting like an idiot lately. But then, how can I ever hope to follow an act like Tim Halpern?"

"Oh Sandy, that's not true at all," I assured him, thrilled by what he was telling me. "You're a great act to follow Tim Halpern. You're a person with a real brain, and real interests, and a conscience." I stopped myself before I blurted out what else was on my mind. Somehow, today, Sandy seemed new, exciting, and attractive to me, and yet I was sure he was the same Sandy as always. Maybe he had been there all along. I had just never bothered to look.

Suddenly, I felt his hand reach for mine, and I gripped him back tightly as if this way I could communicate how I felt. As I turned my face to his, our lips met for a sweet lingering kiss, which ended only when we needed to come up for air.

"Now that you're talking to me," I joked, "does that mean you won't write me any more notes or send me any more pictures in study hall? That was my favorite part of school."

"Not at all," he promised, a big smile spreading across his face. He took my hand and we started to walk home, the street lights popping on behind us.

Three exciting First Love from Silhouette romances yours for 15 days—_free!_

If you enjoyed this First Love from Silhouette,® you'll want to read more! These are true-to-life romances about the things that matter most to you now—your friendships, dating, getting along in school, and learning about yourself. The stories could really happen, and the characters are so real they'll seem like friends.

Now you can get 3 First Love from Silhouette romances to look over for 15 days—absolutely free! If you decide not to keep them, simply return them and pay nothing. But if you enjoy them as much as we believe you will, keep them and pay the invoice enclosed with your trial shipment. You'll then become a member of the First Love from Silhouette℠ Book Club and will receive 3 more new First Love from Silhouette romances every month. You'll always be among the first to get them, and you'll never miss a new title. There is no minimum number of books to buy and you can cancel at any time. To receive your 3 books, mail the coupon below today.

First Love from Silhouette® is a service mark and a registered trademark of Simon & Schuster

First Love from Silhouette

THERE'S NOTHING QUITE AS SPECIAL AS A <u>FIRST LOVE.</u>

$1.75 each

1 ☐ NEW BOY IN TOWN
Francis

2 ☐ GIRL IN THE ROUGH
Wunsch

3 ☐ PLEASE LET ME IN
Beckman

4 ☐ SERENADE
Marceau

5 ☐ FLOWERS FOR LISA
Ladd

6 ☐ KATE HERSELF
Erskine

7 ☐ SONGBIRD
Enfield

10 ☐ PLEASE LOVE ME . . .
SOMEBODY Johnson

11 ☐ IT'S MY TURN
Carr

12 ☐ IN MY SISTER'S SHADOW
Dellin

13 ☐ SOMETIME MY LOVE
Ryan

14 ☐ PROMISED KISS
Ladd

15 ☐ SUMMER ROMANCE
Diamond

16 ☐ SOMEONE TO LOVE
Bryan

17 ☐ GOLDEN GIRL
Erskine

18 ☐ WE BELONG TOGETHER
Harper

19 ☐ TOMORROW'S WISH
Ryan

20 ☐ SAY PLEASE!
Francis

21 ☐ TEACH ME TO LOVE
Davis

22 ☐ THAT SPECIAL SUMMER
Kent

$1.95 each

23 ☐ WHEN SEPTEMBER
RETURNS Jones

24 ☐ DREAM LOVER
Treadwell

25 ☐ THE PERSONAL TOUCH
Cooney

26 ☐ A TIME FOR US
Ryan

27 ☐ A SECRET PLACE
Francis

28 ☐ LESSON IN LOVE
West

29 ☐ FOR THE LOVE OF LORI
Ladd

30 ☐ A BOY TO DREAM ABOUT
Quinn

31 ☐ THE FIRST ACT
London

32 ☐ DARE TO LOVE
Bush

33 ☐ YOU AND ME
Johnson

34 ☐ THE PERFECT FIGURE
March

First Love from Silhouette

35 ☐ PEOPLE LIKE US
Haynes

36 ☐ ONE ON ONE
Ketter

37 ☐ LOVE NOTE
Howell

Watch for February's
BE MY VALENTINE
by Elaine Harper
—those kids who won your heart in
LOVE AT FIRST SIGHT are back again!

FIRST LOVE, Department FL/4
1230 Avenue of the Americas
New York, NY 10020

Please send me the books I have checked above. I am enclos-
ing $_____ (please add 50¢ to cover postage and handling.
NYS and NYC residents please add appropriate sales tax).
Send check or money order—no cash or C.O.D.'s please.
Allow six weeks for delivery.

NAME _____

ADDRESS _____

CITY_____STATE/ZIP_____

Look for These New First Love Romances from Silhouette Books Next Month

My Lucky Star

Becka Cassiday

A big house to manage and a bratty little brother was not Stacy's idea of a fun summer —until she hitched her wagon to a star and blasted off to a romantic adventure.

All American Girl

Vanessa Payton

Can Caroline ever enjoy sports, get good grades, be the popular girl her mother wants *and* keep up her exciting new romance with Mark? Well . . . something had to go and she certainly hoped that it wouldn't be Mark. . . .

Be My Valentine

Elaine Harper

More about the characters from LOVE AT FIRST SIGHT, and especially about Janine's old admirer, Todd Roberts, once the class cut-up who radically changes his life style when he meets the beautiful Heidi under unusual and romantic circumstances.